She's here. She's safe.

James closed his eyes with relief. Everything else could be worked out.

A tiny sound from his daughter had him reaching for her, yet he could look at nothing else but the woman walking through the doorway.

Bella. Oh, my love.

The best part was that this was the Bella he'd loved so fiercely, her jeans dirty, her hair windblown. A smile was blooming up out of him. Bella the gardener, the digging-in-the-dirt-makes-me-happy woman who'd made life a roller-coaster ride of unexpected and offbeat pleasures.

His feet began to move, and his heart started racing. "Bella–" He would grab her, swing her around as he had so many times. He would kiss her until neither of them could breathe, and as soon as he could ditch the kids he would make love to her for hours–

Bella wasn't smiling.

She was scared. Of them. The family she had once adored.

Dear Reader,

Forgiveness...the power of love to overcome...these themes are rich in resonance. I am blessed to experience every day—just as James and Bella have—living with someone I trust to my marrow. But taking this story to the next level, throwing this couple a dilemma they would have said could never happen to them, intrigued me. Does love conquer all? Are some things beyond forgiveness? Is your bond built on a shared past, or would it spark again even if you lost all memory of the life you've lived together?

The EVERLASTING LOVE books offer a chance to examine what happens *after* the happily-ever-after, to go beyond that first flush of new love to explore the challenges and hopes of a long-term relationship. I hope you'll enjoy the ride—and the romance—with James and Bella, as I have.

Thank you for letting me into your hearts and lives to share my stories. I love hearing from readers, either via e-mail at my Web site, www.jeanbrashear.com, or Harlequin's Web site, www.eHarlequin.com, or by postal mail at P.O. Box 3000 #79, Georgetown, TX 78627-3000.

All my best,

Jean Brashear

THE WAY HOME
Jean Brashear

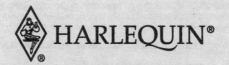

TORONTO • NEW YORK • LONDON
AMSTERDAM • PARIS • SYDNEY • HAMBURG
STOCKHOLM • ATHENS • TOKYO • MILAN • MADRID
PRAGUE • WARSAW • BUDAPEST • AUCKLAND

ISBN-13: 978-0-373-71505-3
ISBN-10:   0-373-71505-6

THE WAY HOME

This is a work of fiction. Names, characters, places and incidents are either the product of the author's imagination or are used fictitiously, and any resemblance to actual persons, living or dead, business establishments, events or locales is entirely coincidental.

This edition published by arrangement with Harlequin Books S.A.

www.eHarlequin.com

Printed in U.S.A.

ABOUT THE AUTHOR

Two RITA® Award nominations, a *Romantic Times BOOKreviews* Series Storyteller of the Year and numerous other awards have all been huge thrills for Jean, but hearing from readers is a special joy. She would not lay claim to being a true gardener like Bella, but her houseplants are thriving. She does play guitar, though, knows exactly how it feels to have the man you love craft a beautiful piece of furniture with his own hands...and has a special fondness for the scent of wood shavings.

Books by Jean Brashear

HARLEQUIN SUPERROMANCE

1071–WHAT THE HEART WANTS
1105–THE HEALER
1142–THE GOOD DAUGHTER
1190–A REAL HERO
1219–MOST WANTED
1251–COMING HOME
1267–FORGIVENESS
1339–SWEET MERCY
1413–RETURN TO WEST TEXAS
1465–THE VALENTINE GIFT
    "Our Day"

SIGNATURE SELECT SAGA
MERCY

Don't miss any of our special offers. Write to us at the following address for information on our newest releases.

Harlequin Reader Service
U.S.: 3010 Walden Ave., P.O. Box 1325, Buffalo, NY 14269
Canadian: P.O. Box 609, Fort Erie, Ont. L2A 5X3

To Ercel, whose love always lights my way home

THE FIRST DAY

A TICKLE, A WHISPER. A murmuring voice eluding my grasp. My foot stirs to give chase. Soft sheets brush my skin.

I open my eyes to a room I've never seen.

In a house I do not recognize.

In dawn's fragile light, I spot mountains. Shiver as crisp, delicious air wafts through the window screen.

Then I fully awaken, and I remember.

That I am Jane Doe.

And I am lost.

CHAPTER ONE

THE WOMAN SANK to the creaking wooden porch step and soaked in the serenity, rare since she'd first regained consciousness in the small town she'd been told was Lucky Draw, Colorado.

Luck was certainly something she could use.

Still, for the moment, she would be asked no questions, could allow her mind respite from her own. Stop flailing against *Who am I?* and *Where did I come from? Is anyone looking for me?* and simply...rest. Only...be.

The green soothed her, though the tangle of it was a little unsettling. If she weeded over there and planted daisies beneath—

She halted. Was this a piece of the puzzle of Jane Doe? A gardener? Heartened, she followed the thread. Bent forward, rested her chin on folded arms atop her knees.

So what would she do with this jumble? She let her eyes go a bit out of focus and imagined the johnsongrass rooted out—though God knows it was as nasty as kudzu to control, with its roots that stubbornly cling to the soil like a toddler to her mama—

She sat up, breathless. Where did kudzu grow?

The faintest of shadows. A wisp of memory, a garden, teased at the edge of her inner vision. Something blue, leggy, a fluff of blossoms at the end of a long stalk.

She frowned, bore down, desperate not to let the image slip away.

But the fragment had already vanished. Frustration soured the brief, earlier bliss, and the bitter edge of fear threatened to drag her back into despair.

A faint buzz snatched her attention. A hummingbird hovered in front of her perhaps five feet away, pretty ruby throat and incessant search for energy, as if he wondered whether she was a flower from which he might drink.

The sight of him calmed her. Staved off fear once more.

She needed to act, to seize control. Perhaps she would plant flowers for her busy little friend. "Thank you," she murmured, to the bird, to the green, to the morning she was, after all, alive to experience, a grace note in this dark hole that was the past she could not recall.

One step, minuscule but desperately appreciated, into the new life she must create.

Strengthened a bit against the constant drain of worry, Jane Doe rose and walked into the chaos that could become a garden, trailing her fingers over the feathery tops of doomed johnsongrass as she formulated plans for how she would spend this first day in the garage apartment Dr. Lincoln—Sam, she corrected—had insisted she make her home, since she had no money and nowhere to go. This tiny village of three hundred fifty-six souls was nearly five hundred miles from the nearest city, with no social services available except the old-fashioned concept of community. After being released from the hospital in Denver, where an MRI had revealed no brain damage beyond this amnesia, she'd accepted Sam's offer because he was a kind man and because she'd had no choice—but only, she reminded him, until her memory returned.

Until she figured out where home really was.

The sheriff had taken her fingerprints and a photo he was comparing with national databases for missing persons, but thus far, he'd come up with nothing. To be so adrift was beyond frightening.

Why isn't anyone searching for me? Am I alone? Is there no one who cares that I'm absent?

I don't know, I don't know, I don't know…anything. But, she reminded herself, that wasn't strictly true. A mirror had shown that she had black, curly hair, shoulder-length and sprinkled with streaks of silver. Green eyes. She was tall for a woman, five foot nine, they'd measured her. Not skinny, but not overweight, either. Probably fiftyish, no longer young but hardly old. She'd borne no children, Sam had told her.

Two dental fillings and pierced ears. Size nine feet. The battered remains of a manicure she was hesitant to remove, only because it was a link of some sort to who she had been.

Serious gardeners didn't get manicures, and her nails were her own, long and sleek beneath the traces of polish. So she probably didn't do manual labor, either, or health care or child care or culinary pursuits. Did she work with her mind? She possessed a quick one, they'd discovered, once she'd regained consciousness. She was good at math, better at writing, and understood some Spanish and a smattering of French.

And she still possessed bruises—she'd fought someone, the sheriff had told her, judging from the skin cells that had been trapped beneath her nails. Her coma of six days had been obtained from a blow to the head during some sort of attack, possibly a carjacking, since she'd been found with no purse and no vehicle, left for dead on the side of a deserted mountain road.

She hadn't, thank God, been raped, Sam had assured her. Though she couldn't remember any of the experience, so would that have mattered? Could you be traumatized by something you didn't recall?

Was there a man in her life who would miss her? Did he wonder where she was? Did he worry?

"Morning." Sam rounded the corner, two mugs in his hands. "Do you like anything in your coffee?"

"How would I know?" But she forced herself to smile. "Sorry."

He shrugged one broad shoulder, then handed her

a mug. "Most likely you will, at some point. As the specialists told us, you may never recover details of the immediate trauma, but over time, the rest of your memory should come back."

"But you can't promise that."

"No," he said. "However, I can and will make sure you have a safe place to heal. There's no rush," he said gently.

But the urgency inside her dictated otherwise. To avoid being ungracious, she ventured a sip.

Then wrinkled her nose.

He grinned. "Too strong for you? Got into the habit in med school— I drink it thick enough to stand a spoon in."

She was very aware that she wore only a borrowed cotton nightgown, covered by an ancient blue man's sweater she'd found on a hook by the door. "I should go change."

"Not on my account." He winked, laughter in the kind chocolate eyes that were her first waking memory. He wasn't a lot taller than her, maybe six feet, a burly teddy bear of a man who commanded both respect and affection from everyone she'd encountered so far, both in Lucky Draw and in Denver. She didn't know what she would have done without his steady, calm guidance in the first awful days when she'd realized just how alone she was. She hadn't thought of him as a man then but as her rock, her guide, her shelter. Her friend.

But Sam was a male, and something inside her held back, as if she was already bound.

She glanced at her left hand. No ring.

"You can't be certain," he said, as if he'd read her mind. "Now, if only marriage involved tattoos..."

She smiled. "Have you ever been married, Sam?"

"Me? No. Never found the right woman. Well..." A shake of the head. "No."

"A little amnesia of your own?"

He grinned. "There was this one weekend in Vegas, but I'm pretty sure it wasn't legal. Here—" He laughed at his joke while digging in his pockets. "Maybe this will make the coffee more palatable. I've got real sugar and the blue stuff and the pink stuff—"

"No yellow packets?"

They stared at each other.

"I like the yellow packets," she said, a smile blooming inside her. "And cream."

"'O ye of little faith.' Didn't I tell you, Jane? One memory at a time."

"I thought of a flower this morning, a blue one, but not its name." She stepped forward. "And kudzu, Sam. Where does kudzu grow?"

"You're asking me? I barely recognize grass." He wrinkled his forehead. "I believe I've heard of it in connection with the South, which would fit with your accent."

"I have an accent?" Until now, she hadn't registered the differences in their speech.

"Maybe you're a Georgia peach or a Mississippi magnolia." He grinned.

"Or just a redneck."

"Nope." He reached for her hand. "No calluses or blisters, for one thing. Those are lily-white, lady hands." He frowned and looked closer. "But you might have played guitar, though not recently."

"What makes you say that?" She pulled her fingers up to her face.

"Feel it. Just the smallest thickening on the tips— guitar players have calluses on one hand, from holding down the strings."

She flexed her fingers without thinking. Closed her eyes to see if anything stirred.

Nothing. Her shoulders rounded.

"Hey," he said softly. "Don't push it. Your brain isn't ready."

I'm ready, she wanted to shout. To scream. But none of this was Sam's fault.

"I, uh, I need to get to the clinic, but I can switch some things if you'd like me to stay around. Or you could accompany me."

The kindness in his voice had her halfway to tears. She sniffed them back. "No." She glanced up. "I'll be fine. Thank you for letting me stay here, Sam. I can't imagine what I would have done if you—"

"You're not alone, Jane. Let yourself rest and recover your strength." He paused. "Anything I can bring you when I return?"

My name, she thought. *I'm not Jane.* But she only smiled and shook her head. "Thanks for the coffee. Have a great day."

But still he hesitated. "You'll be all right here, you're sure?"

"I will. Don't worry."

She would be doing enough of that for both of them.

CHAPTER TWO

Parker's Ridge, Alabama

IF YOU'RE SLEEPING on the couch, so am I.

James Parker paused in the act of forming a perfect Windsor knot in his tasteful tie, remembering the wild black curls of the woman who'd turned his life upside down over thirty-five years ago. The woman who never did the expected, just like that night when they'd had their first big fight. He'd stormed off to sleep on the couch.

She'd chased him down.

Oh, Bella. How did we get from there to here?

And when are you coming back?

His shoulders sagged as he stared at himself in the mirror. He wasn't twenty-five anymore, as he'd been when they'd had that ridiculous argument, the subject of which he couldn't even recall.

But he could still remember the make-up sex, the laughter…the night they'd spent camping out on the living-room floor, surrounded by candles. Because Bella had feared she and he would get stuffy and rigid if they forgot the passion and magic that had brought them together.

Promise me we'll always play, James. My serious James, she'd said fondly, trailing one slender finger over his jaw, studying him with stars in the green eyes that had bewitched him the first second he'd met her. *I'll make sure you take time. We'll be crazy ol' coots when we're old, and we'll always have fun. Life doesn't have to be so serious, you know.*

She'd blown into his practical, ordered existence like a cyclone, and he'd barely kept his feet. A gypsy, a free spirit, his hippie chick had scandalized his family, horrified and fascinated his friends.

He'd never looked back. Never needed more than her.

But the fifty-eight-year-old businessman he saw in the mirror, though fit and trim and still in possession of a good head of hair, blond going silver, had not only lost the art of playing long ago.

Somehow, his wild and crazy Isabella Rosaline had lost it, too.

The ring of the phone jolted him. "Hello?"

"Daddy, why isn't Mama home yet?" His daughter, Cele, seldom bothered with small talk. "Does she sound okay when she calls you?"

He paused. How did he answer that? *I don't know because she hasn't phoned? Because she's trying to decide if she's leaving me?*

What level of honesty did you owe your children when they were grown?

"She wanted some quiet time, honey. I don't expect to hear from her until she's ready to come home." *If* she comes home. *How long are you going to leave me hanging, Bella? I screwed up, all right? But what about—*

"She's been gone two weeks. What about her real-estate business? She had a couple of big deals in the works. How can she afford to be away?"

"Her assistant is competent, Cele. Kara handled things fine when your mother and I went to Aspen."

"That was five days, and Kara said Mama called a dozen times." He heard her intake of breath. "Is everything all right, Daddy?"

Cele might move through life double time, but she was also very intuitive.

Just like her mother.

"Everything's fine, honey. Your mom has been working too hard, that's all. She's overdue for a break." That, at least, was God's honest truth. Bella the homemaker, the earth mother, had morphed into a sleek and formidable real-estate broker, and a very successful one at that.

But he missed his hippie chick, however often her unconventional approach to life had caused lifted eyebrows in his world. When had the change begun exactly? When Cele and Cameron left the nest?

And why hadn't he recognized what was happening sooner?

"It's not like her, Daddy. I'm afraid something's wrong."

His daughter's words crystallized the uneasiness that had been dogging him, and he went stock-still, his fingers tightening on the phone.

Was it possible? Had he been so caught up in his guilt, in his own emotional whirlwind, that he hadn't stopped to realize there might be another explanation for Bella's absence besides how upset she'd been?

"I'm sure she's fine," he said in that parental instinct to soothe and protect. Bella was a strong, resourceful woman.

Who didn't seem to need him anymore.

"She's not answering her cell."

True, but he'd thought she was simply ignoring him. He'd almost been relieved when she hadn't answered, because he still had no idea what to say after the way they'd parted.

Urgency roared to life within him. "She hasn't called Kara, either?" And why hadn't he checked with Kara, except that he'd feared her assistant understood why Bella had left.

"Not once. I'm getting scared." At twenty-three, Cele was small in stature, barely five foot two, her stature belying her strength of will. But now his exceptionally capable and driven daughter suddenly sounded eight years old.

He pictured the gamine features, so delicate beneath the cap of short blond hair, caramel eyes worried. "I'm sure everything's all right, sweetheart, but I'll keep trying your mother." He didn't want to allow even a hint of the sudden cramping in his gut to creep into his voice. The mere thought of Bella hurt or—

"Will you go to the police?"

He wanted to say no, to dismiss the notion as foolish. "If I don't make contact this morning, yes. But only as a precaution. She's probably reading a good book and forgot to turn on her phone. You know how she can be when she's engrossed in a story." And for a moment, he could picture her just that way, long legs curled beneath her.

Except that she hadn't taken time for anything but work in months.

A huge fist of fear clenched his heart. What if she wasn't simply angry but injured or—

Bella. Oh God, Bella. Where on earth are you?

"I'll call you later, honey."

"I'll talk to Cam." Cele's voice quavered just a little, then she firmed it. "I bet you're right. We'll have a good laugh about it later. Add it to our share of Mama stories."

"Yeah." Bella's unconventional behavior and unique view of the world had been a never-ending source of colorful anecdotes, providing hours of teasing when the four of them gathered.

But she hadn't been spontaneous in a very long time.

A boulder-size lump jammed his throat, and it was all he could do to remind himself that there was every reason to hope Bella was simply off some-where, sulking.

The Bella he'd loved didn't sulk, though; she

raged. Swore in two languages and threw dishes at the wall. Then cleaned them up cheerfully, with a toss of that wealth of ringlets, singing as she swept.

But the Bella of the past few years hadn't lost her temper. Hadn't sung.

And he hadn't noticed. "I have to go. I'll catch you later." James clicked off the receiver, waited a few seconds, then dialed.

Her phone went straight to voice mail. Again.

"Bella...baby..." His voice caught, and he nearly disconnected but didn't. "I'm sorry. So sorry. If you won't talk to me, call the kids, please." He paused and squeezed his eyes shut.

"I love—" The tone sounded, cutting off whatever else he would have said. Even if he'd known what that should be. Receiver gripped in one white-knuckled hand, James Parker bowed his head and murmured the only words he could think to utter.

Please. Let her be safe. Let her be mad as hell if she wants—that's okay. Just please...keep her from harm.

Then, with a deep inhalation, he gathered himself and punched numbers into the phone.

"I have to talk to someone. I think my wife might be missing."

CHAPTER THREE

FRESH FROM THE BATH, Jane began rolling her hair into a severe French twist before she realized she had no pins to secure it. Her arms fell to her sides, and she peered into the mirror, frowning at the mass of curls she saw there. How could anyone ever expect to tame it?

And why, she thought as she lifted her hair by the handful, then let it fall, would you want to? She shook her head experimentally and watched the ringlets bounce. What a mess.

I love that mess. It's your glory.

Her eyes widened. She whirled to see the man who had spoken.

But she was still alone. So very alone. She shivered and clutched at her upper arms. Who was he, that voice? Was he a memory, or had her mind begun playing new tricks?

I need my life. Need to know if anyone's there, missing me. Loving me. Does anyone know I'm gone?

Why aren't you searching for me?

Please, someone look for me. I don't want to be Jane Doe.

She halted her pacing. Shrank into her crossed arms while she felt around in her head, as if for a sore tooth. Shouldn't a name be so essential that you would sense when it was right?

She closed her eyes, focused hard. *Who am I? What's my name?*

Who is that man who loves my messy hair?

Don't try so hard, Sam kept saying.

With effort, she let her mind slip into Neutral, to relax and glide, to dance and skim—

She began to twirl in soft, slow circles, to sway from side to side, to hum first faintly, then gathering in strength. Her arms unfolded, reached out. She bared her chest and opened her heart, letting music and motion swell within her. The melody grew faster. She sang louder and twirled and twirled, out into the sunlight, off the porch and into the tangle of green until the warm glow eased her grief, helped her remember that she was alive, if lost. Awake in a new day that smelled fresh and crisp and clean—

"Bella—"

She halted in midtwirl. "What did you say?"

A woman, tiny and ancient, peered at her from the porch of Sam's house. *"Bella.* Italian for beauty. You make a picture in the morning light, signora." She stepped off the porch, smiling. "I am Luisa Ruggino. You must be Jane."

The housekeeper. Her heart thumped in her ears. Must be the unaccustomed exertion making her feel light-headed. "No."

"But Dr. Sam—"

"I mean, yes, that's what they call me, but that's not who I am."

"I agree. Jane Doe is too pale for a colorful creature such as yourself. You should be wearing bold hues."

Colorful creature? She glanced down at her cast-off dress, courtesy of the Methodist Church disaster supplies. A washed-out blue, nearly ankle length, too tight in the bust and far from stylish, but the clothes she'd been wearing when they'd found her had had to be cut off, she was told.

Where were they? Did they hold clues?

"I'd rather have a name. My own."

"Until you remember it, pick one. Ignorance can be an advantage, you see—you may become who-ever you wish."

She was struck by the notion. She could mourn the loss of an identity, a life, a home…or she could seize an opportunity few were granted. Who would you be if you had no ties to a past, a family…

Her knees went weak. Maybe she'd had no children, but was there no one waiting for her?

I love that mess. It's your glory.

"I want to know who I was. Who I am."

The old woman clucked her tongue. "You will, *bella,* probably too soon. And then you will have wasted this precious interlude when you are free as few are." She gestured toward the house. "Follow me. We will find out if you can cook, and meanwhile, you will be too busy to be sad. We shall discover the answer to one piece of the puzzle, and while we work, we will discuss suitable names." She turned away as if assuming Jane would follow. Then she glanced over her shoulder and winked. "Unless, of course, you would prefer to dance in the sunshine a little longer."

"No," she said hastily. "I'd rather be busy."

"A good answer." The old woman walked off without waiting for her.

THE SMOOTH RED GLOBE felt wonderful against her palm. She held it to her nose and sniffed, then turned. "This tomato is fresh picked."

"You know food. Do you also like to garden?"

"I think so." She frowned at her hesitation. It was time to begin building. "Yes. Did you grow this?"

"My house is not far away. See for yourself."

"I'd like that."

"*Buon.* I have produce yet to put up."

"But…" She paused. *Why can't I? What else do I have to do with myself?* She smiled. "I'd love to."

A nod. "Good for you, *bella.* Better to keep the hands busy. It soothes the mind. Now—we will make marinara sauce. How do you remove the skins?" Like a little bird, Luisa cocked her head, dark eyes bright and curious.

Jane frowned.

"No matter. Here—" Luisa handed her a large pot. "Fill this with water and bring to a boil. You drop them in for a minute or two, then—"

"Then put them into cold water," Jane interrupted. "The skin will slide right off." She felt like celebrating.

Luisa was smiling right back at her. "Ah. You are indeed a cook."

"Am I?" Abruptly, her joy receded. "But what does that matter? It gets me no closer to learning whether someone misses me."

"The young are always in such a hurry."

"Young?" Jane held out her hands, examined the backs of them. "I'm hardly that." She let them fall at her sides. "Why did this happen, Luisa? Am I a bad person? Is this a punishment?"

"You are indeed young if you do not understand that there are no tidy answers in life."

"But…" The protest died on her lips. This woman had shown her kindness, yet she was rewarding Luisa with impatience and frustration and impossible questions.

Begin as you mean to go on. She had no idea where that sentiment originated, but she appreciated the innate logic of it. Perhaps her memory would return—God, she hoped so—but if it didn't, was this who she wanted to become—a malcontent, an ingrate?

The people of Lucky Draw had been good to her, had sheltered her when others might have shuffled her off to some social-service agency and washed their hands of her. She'd drawn at least one lucky card in Sam, another in Luisa. There was a world of things she didn't know, but she was fairly certain many people had far less than two friends and several kind acquaintances, a roof over her head and clothes, however few, on her back.

Luisa had a point. She could become—for a time, at least—whoever she wished. She was free of much that others would give a lot to shed—maybe no ties but also no burdens; perhaps no past, but no bad memories, either.

She straightened her shoulders, lifted her head high and proud. "I apologize. You've been nothing but kind, and I've been petulant. Maybe we could start over." She held out a hand. "Hi, there. I'm not Jane Doe."

Luisa grinned. "No, you are not." She shook hands. "So who would you like to be?"

"That's a very big decision." She tilted her head. "What name would you choose if you weren't Luisa?"

For the first time, the old woman seemed uncertain. "Now, there you have me at a disadvantage. It is very difficult to imagine oneself as different." She tapped one finger on her chin. "When I was a little girl, though, I wanted to be called Sophia."

"Why?"

"Pah. Who can say what is in the mind of a child? I hadn't thought of that in years."

"It's a lovely name."

Her eyes narrowed. "You have a world of choices, *bella,* but Sophia would suit you." She winked. "Think of Sophia Loren. You are voluptuous, too."

"Oddly enough, I do know who she is." Refusing to give in to self-pity about that fact, Jane instead glanced down. "I wouldn't make a fashion model, that's for sure."

"Pah—" Luisa waved off the notion. "Stick figures. Real women have hips." She slapped her own. "A true man wants a woman he can get a grip on, my Romeo always told me." Mischief twinkled.

"Your husband?"

"Yes, my beloved Romeo Cesare Ruggino, God rest his soul." She crossed herself.

"Sounds like a film star."

"Oh, he was a handsome devil, that is certain. When you pay me a visit, I will show you a picture."

"I'd like that."

"So you will make a list of possible names, not—Jane?"

She shook her head. "Nope." She was intrigued by the possibilities. "I think I'll audition them. Beginning with Sophia."

A wide smile spread over Luisa's round face. "Auditioning names." She giggled. "Why not?" She winked. "Very well, then, Sophia. But you will be no pampered film star. You will work for your supper."

"Okay." The notion of being useful and not merely lost felt very good. She began filling the big pot with water, and as she did, a vision of smooth green leaves appeared. "Basil."

"What, *bella*—er, Sophia?"

"We need basil. Do you have it?"

Luisa smiled and nodded. "And what else?"

Jane who was now Sophia stared out the window.

"Garlic and onions…oregano. Salt, but I prefer kosher." Her heart thumped once. "Fresh-ground peppercorns. And…extra virgin olive oil. Cold-pressed." She faced Luisa. "Am I right?" she whispered.

"Perfectly."

She peered over the edge of a precipice from which she could either retreat or fly…or fall.

Sophia swallowed hard. And walked to the stove to begin whatever life this would become.

CHAPTER FOUR

JAMES SAT in Bella's garden, once lush and glorious but now overgrown and neglected.

However much money he'd made—and there'd been plenty—she'd still insisted she didn't require help to grow not only her own flowers but vegetables and herbs, here in this upscale neighborhood where most wives played tennis or shopped.

Not for her the diamond tennis bracelets or personal trainers. Bella's muscles were won the hard way—with a shovel and trowel or on long walks where she was just as likely to spot a native plant to adopt.

How long had it been since Bella had set off on one of her rambles?

When was the last time he'd joined her?

Look, she'd say. *See the finches? Hear the mockingbird? What must it be like to fly so free?*

Is that what she'd done—flown away from him, from the life he'd labored so hard to create for them? The life she'd urged him to flee so many years ago?

Don't go to the office today, James. You're the

boss. You can decide when to take off. Let's play
hooky. I'll make a picnic. We'll hike up to the falls.

He'd wanted to. God, how he had. Sometimes he
missed being carefree kids so much, but you couldn't
turn back time. He'd tried leaving all this behind, had
given up a guaranteed future to have her. Worked a
series of menial jobs to the dismay of his family,
who'd been horrified by his choice of mate. He'd
busted his butt to show them how wrong they were
when they'd predicted she'd be the ruin of him, that
he was throwing away a future others would do
anything to possess.

But Bella hadn't wanted that future. Hadn't
cared about a big house or fancy cars. They were
chains that killed the soul, she'd said, and she'd
painted a picture of a good life, a simple one that
the pursuit of wealth would poison. She'd asked
for nothing but his love.

He'd discovered, however, that he was too ambi-
tious for that. He longed to pamper her, to give her
safety and ease and comfort to go with that love.

And so he'd convinced her to return to Parker's
Ridge to claim his heritage. Now he had responsibilities and obligations. When you were the boss,
you couldn't just leave. There were appointments
and meetings and payroll and an example to set.

Always something to get between himself and the
woman who had fascinated him from the very beginning. He remembered that day vividly.

He'd had a fight with his very possessive girlfriend. Usually, he had patience with Beth's moods and could laugh off the short leash she kept trying to put on him. They were the golden couple of Parker's Ridge High School, and his life was pretty well laid out for him, anyway—college at Auburn, then joining the family furniture-manufacturing firm. He drifted along with the plan because none of it bothered him. Lots of his fellow students would sell their souls to have his advantages.

But every once in a while, if he really thought about what lay ahead, he could barely breathe.

He'd stalked from the high-school lunchroom, desperate to get outside. Once on the rolling green grounds, he kept walking until he reached a spreading oak that would provide some shelter and separation. He dropped his books on the grass and collapsed next to them, leaning back against the wide trunk. He closed his eyes for a minute or two, then slid to lie full-length in the peaceful shade.

An acorn dropped onto his belly and bounced off. Then another that he brushed away.

One more had him frowning and looking upward—

Where about a mile of long, shapely legs dangled from a limb just above him—

A hand held out another acorn, ready to release it—

And green eyes sparkled with mischief above lips curved in a daredevil smile. It was the new girl, the one Beth had snubbed just that morning. "Think you can catch this one, Prince Charming? Oh—but that wasn't Cinderella with you earlier, was it? Cruella de Vil, perhaps, in her teenage years?"

He rose and couldn't help but chuckle. The comparison was too apt. "Beth has her moments."

"What are you doing outside the castle walls, Prince?"

"I'm no prince. My name's James. James Parker," he added belatedly, mesmerized by the swinging of those very fine legs beneath a rucked-up skirt that barely covered the essentials.

"Hotshot on campus, I hear. Quarterback, champion debater and king in training." But she winked and didn't seem overly impressed.

Her sense of fun was irresistible. He took a cue from her and sketched a bow. "At your service, *mademoiselle*. And you are…"

"Trouble."

"I'm not afraid of a little trouble."

"But I'm not little." She tilted her head and studied him. "Cocky, are you?"

"Not cocky if you've got the goods."

"Nothing ever rattles you?"

He shrugged. "Nah."

"Well, isn't that just too— Oh!"

She lost purchase, then grasped the limb, only to slip again. He leaped for the nearest branch and began climbing. "Hold on—I'll get you—"

He felt the tree quake, and his heart sped up from fear that he would be too late. He kept climbing but risked one glance…

She was already halfway down from her branch, reaching for the next handhold.

Grinning. Doing quite fine.

Her skirt rode up, and he could see a flash of pink nylon. She climbed onto the branch just above him and, with a mind-blowing glimpse of shapely thigh, eased down beside him. "I warned you."

"That wasn't funny," he said through clenched teeth, his temper in the red zone. She had him way off-balance. He was dying to touch her but oddly afraid to—he didn't know how to deal with any of it.

And she smelled like glory.

"Correction. Not nice, but definitely funny. I've never seen anyone climb a tree so fast, Prince James." Her eyes held mingled laughter and a dare, but she extended a hand. "I'll apologize. You might be more decent than your snotty girlfriend." Behind her bravado he saw something like…loneliness. "I'm Isabella, by the way."

He gripped her hand, but the motion shifted her balance. He caught her against him, and once again, he couldn't breathe, but for a different reason this time. "Hello, Isabella."

Suddenly, though, she turned shy and slipped from his grasp, headed for the ground, pausing at the base only long enough to grab her own stack of books from under a bush.

She glanced back at where he was still frozen in place. "Better not admit we know each other back in there, Prince James. But it was nice meeting you."

She started to go, then revolved. "And thank you for trying to save me." Then she took off before he could say a word.

He watched her go, more than a little tempted to chase her down.

She'd been right the first time. She was capital-T Trouble.

He was mesmerized by her.

Oh, Bella. Tonight, James offered up a wordless entreaty for her safety to whatever being might know where she was.

The police sure didn't. She had left him voluntarily, so without evidence of foul play, there was little they could do. The unspoken message was that maybe she had a reason to stay out of touch, that there might be more to the story of why she'd gone.

He'd given them every bit of information he could imagine they would find useful—forced it on one sympathetic patrolman, actually. Driver's license and social-security number, license-plate number, full description of her vehicle and a packet of photos.

But he was clear that, barring some report of an accident, locating her was up to him. He'd contacted his attorney for a recommendation and was waiting for the private investigator to call.

Meanwhile, he had no idea if Bella was hurt or…

He shook his head violently at the notion. He would not allow himself to even consider that she was lost to him forever.

She was everything to him, the breath in his body,

the marrow of his bones. He'd forgotten that somehow, and they'd slipped from each other's grasp.
Maybe Bella was at fault, maybe he was, perhaps
both.

But he remembered it now, and he could only
pray that he would find her somewhere, safe and
merely angry. Anger he could handle—she had every
right to be furious with him.

*Oh, love, how did we lose each other? How will
we find our way back?*

His cell rang, and he snatched it up. The number
belonged to his office. He cared less than nothing
what might be going on, but he was responsible for
the jobs of hundreds of people who depended upon
him for guidance, for a steady hand at the helm.

James rubbed the bridge of his nose wearily.

And accepted the call.

CHAPTER FIVE

"SOPHIA, IS IT?" Sam bowed over her hand. "This kitchen smells so fantastic that I'll address you as Yankee Doodle if you'll promise to share the food with me." His brown eyes twinkled, but beneath the humor, he looked tired.

"Rough day?"

He ran one palm over his hair. "Probably not over yet. Millie Townsend thinks she's going into labor."

"We'd better get you fed, then. Can't have your hands shaking from hunger, can we, Luisa?" She measured pasta by feel, then dropped it into a pot of boiling water, added a dollop of olive oil and lowered the flame a bit.

"Ah, yes," Luisa said. "You do know your way around a kitchen."

She wrinkled her forehead. "Why do you say that?"

"The oil will prevent the water from boiling over. You added it knowingly, just as you concocted the marinara. And you don't measure. You cook without a recipe. This is—how you say it, Dr. Sam? Not your first rodeo?"

The three of them laughed, and for a moment, she didn't feel so lonely.

"This is how it begins, Jane—er, Sophia," Sam said. "Lacking items from your past to jog your memory, the doctors in Denver said the next best thing is activities you performed before. I've also checked with a few colleagues from my former days at Johns Hopkins about retrograde amnesia. They say—"

"You trained at Johns Hopkins? Isn't that one of the premier medical schools in the country?"

"It is."

"So how did you wind up here?"

"When I could be commanding top dollar in some city, you mean?"

"No. Well, yes, actually."

"I grew up in Massachusetts, and my family is still there. I tried the big-city gig, but it just didn't suit me. I wanted to be closer to the practice of medicine, not spending time in risk-management seminars or playing hospital politics. Plus, I always wanted to see the West. Too many cowboy movies as a kid, probably. And I like the outdoors, so—" he held out his hands "—here I am."

"It's none of my business, really."

"As my patient, arguably it is."

"You're my friend now. I'm healing fine, except—" She tapped her temple.

"The brain is a funny organ, extremely complex and still more mystery than science. With this condition, one might be a world-renowned pianist and would recognize the instrument, perhaps, but not how to play it at first. Yet simple handling of the keys, over time, might bring back pieces of the past—not only the ability to play, but certain events surrounding performances or important people.

"On the other hand, sometimes special people from the past can do more harm than good because they have expectations of the amnesiac based on prior relationships. They remember everything they've ever felt with or about that person, and they respond accordingly, but that response is often too personal and highly uncomfortable for someone who is, in her own mind, meeting them for the first time."

"You're saying that even if I do have loved ones who locate me, I still might not recognize them? I'd feel nothing for them?"

"Possibly."

"But soon I would, right?"

His gaze was troubled. "There's reason to hope."

She couldn't breathe. She'd pinned everything on being found. "Are you saying that I might never regain my memory? That even if someone out there does care about me, nothing will change?" Shaking inside, she set down her spoon and walked to the door.

"*Bella,* do not worry yourself. Everything will turn out right—"

"Jane—I mean, Sophia—" Sam stood. "Sit down. Please."

She swiveled. Blinked back hated tears. "I'm not Jane. I'm not Sophia. I'm not…anyone, and you're telling me—" She clapped one hand over her mouth to stop the torrent of fear and anger. She shoved open the screen and bolted.

"Don't—"

She heard Sam calling, but she couldn't answer. Instead, she ran as hard as she could, ignoring conifer branches that slapped at her, scratched her. She welcomed the pain that mirrored the roar of anguish building inside her.

What if I never—

Oh, God, the prospect was too horrible. She ran and ran, heedless of her surroundings, until she tripped on a rock and went sprawling to the ground in a small clearing. Bruises not yet healed cried out in protest, but they only added to the cacophony within. She had tried to show courage, to be kind, to nurture patience even on the days when she was most terrified. When she thought she couldn't bear one more pitying glance or whispered aside. Of the few things she believed she knew about herself, she'd imagined that she might be strong and at least a little brave.

But here, lying on damp, unfamiliar earth smelling of leaf and mold and tangy branches, injured in both body and soul and more alone than she thought she could endure…

She broke. Sobbed until her chest hurt and her head throbbed from the storm of tears. Her heart ached as she gave up all pretense, relinquished every last shred of hope that out there somewhere was one person who loved her. Who would search the world for her. A faint unease she'd been fighting to ignore murmured that she was on her own, that there was no magical soul mate to trust.

That she had no one but herself, in the final analysis. Whatever life she would weave from the broken strands of who she'd once been must begin here.

She rolled onto her back and peered up through endless green branches darkening to the charcoal of night. Up into fading blue sky streaked with clouds stained coral and gold.

She breathed deeply of the crisp air on the verge of cold, and she forced herself to stretch, to inhale the splendor around her, drawing it into the fibers of her muscles, the ruby rush of her blood.

She was alone, but she was alive. She dwelled— for the moment, at least—in a place of great beauty, and back in the house she had fled were two people who had extended the hand of friendship to her, as well as sustenance and shelter.

Begin as you mean to go on. If only she knew who had said that to her, but that was lost, along with so much else, in the shadows of her mind. Regardless, she had the saying to cling to, a North Star to serve as her guide.

Sam hadn't told her there was no hope, and for an instant, she let herself feel how desperately she yearned for it.

But then she sat up, stretched her arms to the sky and faced the heavens. "Thank you," she said to whatever force had created this loveliness. Had spared her life.

She would do her best not to ask for more. Instead, she rose to her feet and brushed leaves and grass and seed pods from her hair, her skin and her very ugly dress.

And she smiled. She needed her own clothes, so she would find a way to earn the money for them. Sam could definitely use a gardener, even with fall rapidly approaching. And Luisa wasn't getting any younger, so perhaps she could share cooking duties. Preparing food had soothed something inside her nearly as much as contemplating the improvements to Sam's sorry garden had.

Just then, she heard a rustle off to her side.

Sam stood at the edge of the clearing beneath an aspen already mostly gold. "I'm sorry. Most people think I have a good bedside manner, but—" He spread his hands out to his sides.

"The fault isn't yours. I just got…" She stared off to the side. "Overwhelmed."

He approached her. "Anyone would. I promise you that every effort is being made to figure out your identity, except…"

"What?"

He frowned. "We could call in the media, splash your face all over television, newspapers, the Internet, but—"

"Go on."

"It's a lot of pressure on you, and stress is counterproductive for your condition. There'd likely be a horde of strangers descending, plus all the ghouls and con artists we'd have to weed through. Everyone I consulted advised waiting to subject you to that until you were able to decide for yourself."

She smiled past her jitters. "Always so thoughtful of me. You're a wonderful doctor, Sam. A big city's loss is Lucky Draw's gain."

"You're more than welcome." His answering smile was both fond and a little sad. "I just wish…" He shook his head. "Never mind."

She tactfully didn't inquire further. Too much was jumbled up inside her. She didn't know whether she'd ever been married, if there was a man in her life. Sam was a very good man, and an attractive one, but—

"It's getting dark," he said. "And I didn't bring a flashlight with me. We'd best be going." He held out a hand.

She hesitated for a moment, then gratefully accepted it.

They walked in silence back to his house. When they started up the steps of the porch, she decided to press forward. "I need some jeans, Sam."

He glanced at her as if that was the last thing he expected her to say. "I'll buy you some tomorrow."

"Please don't. I'd prefer to purchase my own, but I have to get a job."

"You most certainly do not." He opened the door. "You're my guest."

"No." She halted. "I don't like being company. I have no idea how long I'll be here or if I'm ready yet to encourage that deluge of attention. There's so little

I am sure about, but if I think about the whole big picture, I'll lose what's left of my mind, so—" she shrugged "—I'm not going to. I have to find a way to exert some control." She gestured around her. "This is a nice place. I'm not so afraid here. Being fearful really kind of ticks me off. I have a feeling that I might not be a person who's usually timid."

He grinned. "I'd say you can take that to the bank."

"So I insist on earning my keep. I thought I could tackle your landscaping."

"Or lack thereof."

"Exactly. No English garden—I don't mean that. Nothing manicured. But you could use a space for vegetables, and flowers are good for the soul. You have a few, but they're sadly neglected. It's the wrong time of year, but the soil could be prepped, so—" Then a thought hit her. "But you might not be able to afford to pay me. I'll understand if— Or maybe someone else around here—"

He chuckled. "I did the big-city gig first. I've got a few shekels saved up." He glanced behind her. "Heaven knows you're right about my jungle."

"I could help Luisa cook, too, and I—"

"Jane." He gripped her arms. "Sorry—Sophia—"

"I'm sick of auditioning names already," she interrupted. "Let's go back to Jane. It's simpler."

"If that's what you wish." He slung an arm around her shoulders. "For now, you require rest as much as anything else. Before you sign on to be my jack-of-all-trades, let's just take things slow, okay?"

She fought the urge to cuddle against him, out of relief, out of more of that blasted fear. Or other impulses she wasn't ready to name.

But she couldn't quite stem the tears, so she ducked her head to hide them. "Thank you."

He tilted her chin up. For a moment, she had the sense of the whole world holding its breath, waiting.

Sam exhaled sharply. Shook his head.

And bent to place a kiss on her forehead.

She sighed, too, unsure if it came from disappointment or relief.

"Let's go inside," he said. "You should eat. Doctor's orders."

Confused and tired but also jubilant to have made any sort of start, she only nodded and followed.

CHAPTER SIX

JAMES SHRUGGED OFF his jacket, shoulders sagging. The meeting with the private investigator had been long and grueling. The man was reputed to be the best, but he fell a little short of insulting in his obvious cynicism about whether Bella's continued absence could be attributed to foul play.

James couldn't seem to get through to the man how deeply they'd loved each other—

And the instant he registered the past tense, he was struck by the sight of the wide, empty bed. Desolation swept over him with such force he nearly staggered.

Dear God. He still loved Bella with everything in him.

But he wasn't at all certain that she loved him anymore. This very room echoed with their last exchange, frightening, most of all, because there had been so little heat in it.

"You're packing."

Calmly—too calmly—she'd folded a blouse, tucked it beside other garments. "I thought I'd get away for a bit."

"Good idea. Where shall we go?"

Her shoulders stiffened. Her eyes, when they met his, were empty of any expression, and the dull gong of fear had reverberated within him.

"I need to think, James."

"About what?" But he knew.

Disappointment flickered, but she never said a word.

"Bella. Look at me."

She shook her head.

"Don't do this, sweetheart. We can work things out. We just have to talk."

"I can't discuss this with you. Not after what you've done." She walked to the bathroom. Tried to close the door.

He shoved through. "Bella, you abandoned me first." Agitation sent him pacing. "You're never at home anymore—you're always working. We hardly see each other."

"And you don't even understand why, do you?" Two sharp shakes of the head, and she returned to placing her toiletries in the suitcase. "Do you realize who we've become, James? We're your parents. I'm the Stepford Wife, and you're the bastard who cheats on her." She blinked rapidly. "I don't know which is harder to forgive."

"How many times do I have to say I'm sorry? One slip, Bella, one." He struggled for composure. "It was wrong, so wrong. I still don't know how—"

"It's not only that. It's what's missing. What I can't bear anymore."

"What's missing? I've worked my ass off to give you everything possible. A beautiful home, a life of luxury—"

"You have. And made me a prisoner in it."

"What?" he thundered. "How can you say that? You know I love you."

She glanced at him, and he thought, for a second, that tears glittered. "Once you loved a girl who was different," she murmured, and lifted her bag. "But we're living your life, James, the one you said you didn't want. The one you asked me to make sure you left behind." She touched his cheek, and her eyes were as beautiful as ever but so sad that his own grew damp.

"I don't think I can live this way anymore. Something inside me is dying, and I can't—" Her voice broke, and she spun away.

He grabbed her arm. "Bella, we can fix this. Just tell me what you want and I'll make it happen, but don't leave. Or, let me go with you."

She stood quivering in his grasp, head bowed. "I never thought I'd say these words, but..." She glanced back over her shoulder. "I don't want you with me, James. At least, not right now. And if you love me, you'll let me go."

"For how long?" He could barely choke out the question.

"I don't know."

"Bella, this is crazy. We belong together. We always have."

Her eyes filled then. "I thought that was true."

"It is, damn it. You know it is. Bella, you can't go. How can we repair anything if you're not here?"

"Not everything is a puzzle to be solved. Sometimes there are no clear answers." She smiled at him then, through tears rolling down her cheeks. "Logic can't fix this."

"Love can, damn it. How can you just walk away? How can you leave me?"

"Please," she whispered.

Fury and fear rendered his voice harsh. "Go ahead, then. You've got your mind made up. You don't really care what this does to us, do you?"

She held herself very straight as she walked slowly to the door. "I'm doing this for us, James. For what we once were." She bit her lip. "Be well, my love."

And then he uttered the words he wished daily, hourly, he could retract.

"If you leave now, Bella, there may be nothing for you to come back to," he roared as she vanished from sight.

He'd listened, over and over, both in dreams and waking, for the faintest murmur of a response from her, but as far as he knew, Bella had left him with only his angry threats ringing in her ears.

He sagged onto the mattress and buried his face in his hands.

Then he rose from the bed they'd shared so many nights, and left the room that had once been their haven. At the doorway, he stopped, viewing it all as if for the first time, and contrasting the impeccable good taste of cool, muted shades and pricey antiques, with the bedrooms of their early days, brimming with flamboyant paisley hangings, eye-popping batik furniture covers, macramé tables and plants everywhere, most of which she'd grown herself from cuttings and seeds obtained free.

Something inside me is dying.

The evidence had been before him all along—the home that might as well have been his mother's, the clothing she wore that no longer bore the mark of the magpie.

Bella. I remember the girl you were. How much I loved her. What sparkle she brought to my life.

I swear that when I find you, I will spend the rest of my days nurturing whatever is left of her within you.

And I will find you.

Knowing he would not sleep this night, that he couldn't stand to be in this bed without her again, James strode down the stairs to his office. He would tie up his own loose ends, so that the moment he found out where Bella was, he could responsibly leave to go after her.

People depended on him to be steady, and however rocky he felt, he would do his best by them.

But if push came to shove, Bella was his first priority. Too often in the past, she hadn't been.

To the end of his days, he would regret that.

THE NIGHT CREPT IN through the window, tree branches chattering against the hoot of an owl. She drew her new fleece robe around her. Soon the ever-present wind would be cold and snow would fall.

Would she still be here? Or would her memory have returned and she would be certain where she belonged?

Belong. She clasped the word to her bosom, attempting to imagine how that felt. How did you know where you were meant to be? Lucky Draw was becoming more familiar by the day and some of its three hundred or so residents evolving into what might be friends.

What was a friend? Did she have any in that life she'd left behind?

Why had she gone? Had she chosen to be alone, so far from the South from which her accent indicated she had come? Or was she a transplant who now lived nearby, and she was only slightly off her chosen path? The questions circled her like raptors, each one seeking the moment when fear rendered her vulnerable to a deadly strike.

But more than anything, she could not afford to be weak. If darkness and solitude enervated her, made her want to lie down and weep, then they must be avoided at all costs. She would remain busy from morning until night, until she was so exhausted that sleep would overtake her without this dreaded time when longing pierced her to the heart, sliced away what little armor she could manage.

She could try being aloof and silent, she supposed, but within her was a tearing, agonizing need for connection. To reach out; to have a hand to hold, a shoulder to lean on. Someone who'd known her as a girl, who'd cherished her as a woman.

And someone, lots of someones, for her to love.

Suddenly, she had the sensation of a baby's head beneath her hand, of stroking fine hair, dark and straight. A tender part revealed pale skin, and as her hand moved downward, she touched a small ear, a cheek, a chin—

Breathless, she bit her lip and waited for more.

Mama. A voice, young and adoring.

She closed her eyes and focused hard.

One glimpse of brown eyes, and—

Nothing.

She shook her head. "No," she moaned. Extended her hand to recapture—

Gone.

The rush of love bowled her over. Knocked her legs right out from under her, and she sank to the floor, head bowed, gripping her fingers for fear the memory would be lost once more.

Mama. The child's voice echoed in her head. She squeezed her eyes to prevent the face from drifting away.

Don't leave me, baby. Please don't...

On her knees, she rocked, her arms empty beyond bearing, her heart full and aching. For an instant, she thought she could feel a bundle of blankets.

Could see a man's hand cradling the tiny head, fingers brushing her breast. Feel sunshine and joy pouring from her to him and back, through the body of this child.

More, please…oh, please, please…let me see more.

Long after the images had faded and she was alone again, she remained hunched over her imaginary burden, rocking and sobbing with a desperate yearning flooding her chest. The night surrounded her again, and she came to herself in this place that no longer felt familiar, only strange and…wrong.

Even as the loneliness overpowered her—

Hope, faint as breath, flickered to life.

She had loved. Had been loved.

And she'd had a memory of a life, if confusing. The child's voice was too old for the infant's face. Were they the same person?

Urgency zinged through her. She must write this down, keep every snippet, for surely—oh, please, God, surely—there would be more. And somehow, she would piece them together and find out where she belonged.

Frantically, she searched the apartment, but neither she nor Sam had thought about having pen and paper here. She glanced at the clock: 3:00 a.m. Her gaze darted toward the house. Sam would be sleeping. He needed his rest.

So did she, but she was terrified to lie down, for fear she would forget. That the endless void would swallow this precious clue.

Sam would understand, she thought.

She charged through the door on winged feet and

charged down the stairs, across the yard. "Sam—" She pounded on the backdoor, all the while clutching at each detail, over and over again. "Sam, wake up—"

Footsteps thundered. Sam yanked the door open. "What's wrong? Are you hurt? Are you—" He pulled her inside, scanned her from head to foot.

"No. I'm fine, I'm okay. Sam, I need paper, a pen—" She raced to the pad she knew he kept by the phone, crying and laughing at the same time.

"What?" His voice was rough from sleep. "Why?"

She found the supplies. "I remembered something. I have to write it down before—"

He shook his head as if to clear it. "That's great. What was it?"

She paused in her scribbling, feeling a smile stretch wide. "A child." Tears began again as wonder overcame her. "Sam…oh, Sam, I think I have a child."

He stood there, blinking in the light.

"You said I hadn't given birth, but I could have adopted, couldn't I? Oh, God, Sam, it was wonderful and terrible at the same time. I heard a voice. I could feel the hair." She halted. "I saw a swaddled infant, and—" Her head lifted abruptly as a new detail emerged. "And a man's hand, Sam. Cradling the baby's head, and we were happy—oh, beyond happy. We were a family, Sam, the three of us, and I felt so much love."

Pain swamped her then. Despair. "Where are they?" She looked up at him. "Why aren't they searching for me?" Then the thought struck her, and she couldn't breathe. "Oh, God, what if I'm the only one left? What if—" She bent double from the agony.

Sam's arms closed around her. "Shh. Take a deep breath, Jane. We'll locate them, I promise. You don't know enough right now, but…"

"It's time, Sam. Splash my picture all over everywhere. I need them to find me. Whatever that requires."

"Jane—"

"No, Sam, don't argue. I have a family. Please—" She faced him. "Please help me."

"I don't like it, but I said it would be your decision, once you were stronger. I'm warning you, though, I'm going to monitor you. I know you're impatient to get back to your life, but I will not allow you to compromise your health."

"I understand. Thank you, Sam."

"Okay." He raked fingers through his hair and yawned. "I'll go call the sheriff."

She pressed her lips together, fighting the anxiety that gripped her. "Get some sleep. It can wait until dawn. I'll just go back and write everything down."

"You sure?"

"Yes. I'm sorry I woke you."

"Jane, I can make coffee. We can talk."

She tamped down the urgency. "You should get some sleep. I'll be fine."

"You rest, too, okay?"

Not likely, she thought. But she smiled to put him at ease. "Sure thing. See you in the morning."

"Jane—"

She glanced back over her shoulder and noticed his worried expression. "What?"

He shook his head. "Nothing. Please try to rest."

"I'll be fine, Sam. I can handle whatever it is, I promise."

I have to. I want to go home.

CHAPTER SEVEN

JAMES LONGED to be anywhere but here, but this meeting with the bankers was critical to the company's survival, life or death to the needs and dreams of over four hundred employees, their families and the town of Parker's Ridge.

And James struggled to concentrate. Because, suddenly, everything he'd believed true in his life seemed to be a lie.

"Daddy?" Cele bent to him and whispered, "Lloyd just proposed terms for an expansion loan."

James snapped to attention. "Debt is not the answer. This company was built by my great-grandfather on a pay-as-you-go basis. That principle is all that kept us alive in my grandfather's time, during the depression."

"James, we have to expand or this company is doomed. We cannot compete with cheap, assemble-it-yourself composite wood furniture sold over the Internet," his accountant protested.

"Quality, both in materials and craftsmanship, has always been this company's byword," he responded.

"People don't pay for quality anymore. Price is critical—"

"Not always," Cele interrupted. "There is a hunger in this country for things that last. For a sense of heritage that Parker's Ridge symbolizes."

One of the bankers made a scoffing noise, but James held up his hand to quiet the man. "Go on," he urged his daughter.

Cele's cheeks were bright with hectic color. She glanced sideways at him as if seeking reassurance.

He nodded. He'd always hoped, as a man does, that Cameron would choose to follow his footsteps in the family business, but Cameron had been caught in the fever of flight, much as James had once burned to travel the globe. Bella had put her foot down, insisting that James give Cameron his chance. *Don't chain him to the family business, James. Let him fly free, as you once dreamed of doing.*

Unexpectedly, it was his daughter who had shown real interest in Parker's Ridge. She'd majored in business at Vanderbilt and performed so well that she'd had her choice of job offers upon graduation. She'd requested a place with him, instead. Been willing to work her way through the departments these six months or so, storing up information and impressions and posing a million questions.

But never before had she interjected herself, certainly not into discussions as crucial as this one.

That's our little girl, Bella had once said. *She*

watches and studies without ever saying a word, but when she does, it's often extraordinary.

"Please. I'd like to hear more," he said.

"This is a wealthy country," she said, "compared with the rest of the world. A technologically advanced one and an impatient one. It's easy to get used to instant everything—communication, food, transportation, entertainment. You can click a mouse and have a dizzying array of goods at your doorstep the next day." She glanced around the table. "But many among us are exhausted from the 24/7 bombardment of stimuli available."

"We're in the furniture business," Lloyd said with no little impatience.

James saw Cele's knuckles whiten as she formed a fist in her lap. He ignored the skeptical glances around the table and squeezed her hand beneath the table. "We are, Lloyd, and experience leads me to believe that Cele will show us the connection—" he sent the man a quelling glare "—allowed the opportunity."

Others traded glances, but the group subsided for the time being.

"One of the biggest growth areas in retail is found in high-quality goods, preferably handcrafted," Cele told them. "Likewise, young women by the droves have begun to learn to knit, though handmade garments not only require time but are a great deal more expensive than goods made in China, for example, in factories where workers earn pennies a day."

Her voice strengthened even as foreheads beetled.

"On television, cooking shows, sometimes involving complicated and time-consuming recipes, draw a record number of viewers, and young singles form dinner clubs to try out new dishes they've made themselves, again at greater expense of both time and money."

She glanced at James, who was certain that he was not hiding a proud smile all that well. He winked at her, and her eyes reflected gratitude.

"My point is that even for the prime buying demographic of eighteen-to-thirty-five-year-olds who have grown up on microwaves and instant messaging and family schedules so complicated that a shared meal is the exception in most households, there is a hunger for a world they've only heard about, one where you bought from the local merchant who was also a neighbor, and what you bought was made to last. They want some sense of stability in a world that changes so fast none of us can begin to keep up."

She scanned the group. "That nostalgia is exactly what Parker's Ridge can provide them—handcrafted furniture would be one example, for those with the money to afford it, but another market comes from those who can't pay for a one-of-a-kind item but would still relate to a family-owned business with a reputation for quality. Employees who are part of the family, as my father has made the people here. A place where they could see furniture being made, both custom pieces and stock, and experience a small town in the mountains, one rich in artisans and craftspeople and bed-and-breakfasts—a whole experience, a destination.

"We have the raw material here—more than that, actually. We have the reputation my father and his father and grandfather built over years and years. We can turn a negative to a positive by letting go of the notion that we must compete with cheap goods."

Her dark eyes were shining now with the fervor of her convictions, and though she shared no blood with her adoptive mother, James could hear and feel Bella in every word, every gesture. Bella's passion for the handmade, the homegrown, had taken root in her daughter in a manner that would have Bella's buttons bursting.

For a moment, James could barely breathe for missing his wife. Only his love for their daughter kept him in his seat, when his whole being cried out to race from this room and devote all his time to the search for her.

"WE HAVE TO HANDLE this carefully," Sam said, raking fingers through hair that already seemed to have been through an eggbeater. "You're positive you're ready?"

She nodded past her inner quiver. "There's a child out there who might need me." She sighed. "Given my age, I understand intellectually that the child is most likely grown, but in here—" she tapped her chest "—it's only a baby."

It. Why didn't she know instinctively if the infant was a boy or girl? Maybe the child wasn't hers.

But no—she was certain about that, and somehow it was not the baby's head but the man's hand that convinced her. That hand...

Simply the image of it made her feel safe. Cherished.

"Sam, I don't care." She leaned forward. "Whatever I have to go through, I need this. Need them."

His expression was both sad and resigned. For a second, she almost thought—

No. He wasn't getting attached to her. He was not looking at her as a man does a woman.

She sat back in her chair, stunned by the notion. Sam Lincoln was the finest of men, kind and caring. He reached out to those in trouble, that was all. Compassion went deep into his bones, a necessary part of the healer's makeup.

He was at least ten years younger than her. He could not possibly be attracted.

She risked a glance. A man, not a doctor, stared back at her.

She'd have to think about that later. "Take my picture, Sam. Go on, now," she said softly. "I have to know."

Her fingers smoothed over the paper, absently tracing the curved skull of the child, the lean, strong fingers of the man. She'd discovered another piece of herself. She could draw—pretty darn well, as a matter of fact.

She tried to lighten the mood. "Do a better job than the sheriff, okay? His was more like a mug shot."

Sam exhaled, then got to his feet. "All right. Let's go outside where the light is better."

Jane followed suit. Touched her fingertips to his arm gently. "Thank you."

"Let's see if you're so grateful later," he said gruffly. He halted. "But one part is nonnegotiable. No one gets to know where you are. All inquiries have to come through me."

She studied this gentle bear of a man who'd gone the extra mile for her, again and again, and forcibly she restrained her impatience. What was a day or two or even three, in the face of a lifetime? "All right." She smiled and rose to her toes to kiss his cheek. "My Saint George, ready to fight the dragon."

But he didn't smile back. "This might not work, Jane. Don't get your hopes up. I don't want you hurt."

Too late, she thought. But to him, she only nodded. "I have to try."

His sigh was long and low. "I understand." He lifted his camera and snapped one shot before she was ready.

"Hey!"

He grinned. "That one's for me." He pointed to the flower bed she'd worked on all day yesterday. "How about there?"

I could fall for this man, she mused. As she settled in place before the hollyhocks and chrysanthemums, a sudden shiver shook her, and she nearly backed out. What if the image that had come to her was a movie or a dream? How could she know what she would be walking into? What she had here was safe and fine. Maybe she should just wait.

No. She steeled herself and faced the camera.

However safe, this was not her life.

THAT NIGHT, the silent house rebuked him.

Not that James was accustomed to coming home before dark the past several months, and Bella had worked many nights herself. He tried to remember the last time they'd shared an evening meal. She'd had clients to meet and houses to show. He'd had endless spreadsheets and financial reports to comb through, seeking a miracle. His assistant, Julie, had put in long hours, too, working by his side. They'd been a good team, and he'd appreciated having someone to share his worries with, someone who knew the company inside out. Someone who didn't depend on him to put on a brave face.

It had begun with a neck rub. How trite. How goddamn stupid.

He opened the refrigerator and stared inside, attempting to conjure up an appetite.

But thinking about his one fall from grace had curdled his stomach. That it had been only one occasion was cold comfort. That he'd felt like slime immediately after made his crime no less. He hadn't intended it; no, hadn't encouraged Julie. Hadn't, if the truth be told, even realized she had a crush on him.

He'd just been so damn lonely—and scared.

And that might be his greatest sin—that he hadn't sought Bella out, hadn't bared his soul to her. Had entrusted secrets to a virtual stranger instead of the woman who'd been his life.

Do you see who we've become, James? We're your parents. I'm the Stepford Wife, and you're the bastard who cheats on her.

I don't know which is harder to forgive.

Once they'd been so close they practically shared breath. Back in the days when they'd struggled to scrape together enough pennies to buy a cheap bottle of wine or splurge on a fast-food meal.

They'd made it through the dark times, three miscarriages in four years, and the heartache of hopes lifted, only to be dashed soon after. The evenings he'd witness her struggle to smile past her grief while he'd battle back his own despair to comfort her. Days, weeks, months of pain…but they'd endured. Never lost touch.

He closed the refrigerator door, his mind adrift in the past…

BELLA LAY curled in the center of the bed, the shades drawn, casting the space into gloom. He didn't even have to ask what had happened; after three miscarriages and countless monthly disappointments, he knew.

For a second, he prayed for strength…

And the right words, though in truth, there were none.

"James?" She sat up hastily, threw off the afghan

she'd knitted in cloud-soft pastels, the one meant for the first baby, back when they were full of innocence and faith. "I didn't realize what time—"

He settled onto the mattress beside her. "Come here." He drew her onto his lap and wrapped his arms around her. "I'm so sorry," he murmured into her hair.

"It doesn't matter." A shudder went through her, and she gripped his suit coat in both hands.

"It does, sweetheart. It hurts you every time."

"You think I should quit trying." Her voice was muffled by his shoulder.

Yes. No. His eyes burned. He'd wanted to make babies with Bella, to mingle their blood as they'd united their hearts and lives. To raise a big family in a house filled with their love.

They conceived babies, one after another. He and Bella were very fertile, the bounty of their bond expressing itself in creation again and again.

But the tiny lives could never hold on.

And Bella refused to give up on bearing him the heirs she knew he wanted. That she wanted just as much, for different reasons.

Because Bella was all about creation. She gardened, she sewed, she knitted. Painted and played guitar and cooked like a dream. She was the perfect homemaker, in the best sense of that word. Wherever Bella was became a nest, a refuge, a world of color and light and joy.

It was the cruelest of ironies that a woman so clearly meant to have a family and share her abundant love would be denied the chance to do exactly that. There had never been a more natural mother born, he was convinced.

So, heartache after heartache, she continued. And because he could deny her nothing, he went along, each time summoning the strength to help her through at the end.

Because he loved her more than life. Because he would concede her anything.

But maybe love required something different from him now.

"Yes," he said, though the pain of that finality was a sword slicing through his chest. Eyes closed, he held her more tightly. "We don't have to have children for our life to be good, sweetheart. Or—" He watched the dream die, admitting to himself just how much a child of his blood and hers had mattered. How deep in the bone that urge was bred. "We could adopt."

She recoiled, her eyes dark and haunted. "That's not what you want."

He could lie to her, but she'd know. "I've changed my mind."

"Why?"

"Because you mean more."

"But—"

He pressed his fingers over her lips and shook his head. "No buts, honey. This is killing you, and if I lose you, I lose everything."

Her eyes flooded with tears. "James, I'm so sorry. I don't understand why I can't—"

He hushed her with a kiss. "Neither do I, love, but I won't let you torture yourself over it anymore." For a moment, he embraced her, inhaling the scents that clung to her, rosemary and sunshine, honeysuckle and the tang of tomatoes...aromas of earth and sky and this bounteous woman who deserved so much better than he could ever provide her.

She clung to him just as fiercely. "What would I do without you?" she whispered.

"You'll never have to find out." He gripped her, then forced himself to let go. He leaned away and tipped her face to his. "The world is full of children who would bloom under the hands of the best gardener I know. Where shall we start looking?"

The hope that flared was all the answer he needed to be certain he was doing the right thing.

Her fingers stroked the afghan. The sorrow hadn't completely fled her gaze, but her face began to light with the excitement that was, always and ever, the essence of Bella.

Beneath it was a trace of fear. "The agencies will see that we'd make some child happy, won't they, James?"

He defied anyone to do otherwise. He'd fight to his last breath to make certain. "How could they not? No one—" His voice was rough and fierce as he embraced her again. "No one who meets you could possibly doubt that you have enough love in you for the whole world."

"You, too," she murmured into his ear. "You've loved me so well and been so patient with me, even through—"

He shook his head and silenced her with a kiss. "I've done nothing but try to deserve you." His eyes grew moist. "You are everything, Bella. There is nothing I wouldn't do for you."

"I love you so much, James. Oceans deep. Wide as the sky."

"We'll be okay, sweetheart. I promise."

SO YOUNG AND SO BRASH, to believe that he could make the vow, that merely speaking it was enough.

To hold such riches in his hand and manage to lose them and never even notice they were gone—

Until the love of his life walked out the door.

The phone rang, and he leaped for it. His shoulders sagged as he saw his son's number displayed. Bella was so real in his mind that he'd expected it to be her.

"Hello?"

"Hey, Dad. I got my instrument rating today."

Cameron's excitement zipped through the lines. "That's great, son. That's absolutely terrific. Your mother—" He pinched the bridge of his nose and forced himself to continue. "She'll be proud, Cam. Really proud."

"Does that mean…"

James realized his mistake. "No." He let out his breath in a sigh. "I don't know anything." Damn it.

"Why can't the police do something?" For an instant, Cam was a boy, frightened and angry.

"Because she left on her own. For all they know, she's sitting on a beach somewhere."

"What about you, Dad? Where do you think she is?" A pause. "Why did she go, Dad? This isn't like her."

He didn't want to have this conversation. "Cam—"

Just then, the doorbell rang. "Hang on a second, son." He descended the stairs and saw a man in a suit and a uniformed officer waiting. "Cam, I'll have to call you back. Someone's at the door."

"Who?"

His heart sped as he registered the grim expressions on the two men's faces. Whatever this was, he would spare his children as long as possible. "Just a neighbor. I'll talk to you in a little while, okay?" He gripped the knob, reluctant to open the door until Cam was safely away.

"All right, Dad. Bye."

"Goodbye, son." But he didn't click off until after Cameron was gone, feeling an odd need for the connection.

Then he opened the door.

"James Parker?"

"Yes?"

"I'm Detective Gordon, and this is Officer Hunt. May we come inside?"

His chest filled with a sense of doom. "Is this about my wife? Is she all right?" He squeezed his eyes shut for a second, steeling himself for the response.

"Let's sit down, Mr. Parker."

"No." He met the man's gaze. "Tell me now. Don't string it out. Is she—" He could not say the words.

"We don't know where your wife is, Mr. Parker."

"Then why—"

"Her car was discovered in Idaho during a raid on a chop shop."

"Chop shop?" He shook his head. "Idaho?"

"A chop shop is where stolen cars, especially luxury cars like your wife's BMW, are transported to be disassembled for parts."

"But where's Bella? And how did her car get to Idaho?" He confronted the detective. "Now will someone take me seriously when I say that something has happened to her?"

"We have to, after what else was found."

"What?" His throat was tight with fear.

"Bloodstains on the upholstery."

"Blood," he repeated dully. "Oh, God." He grabbed the man's arm. "I'm going to Idaho." He glanced around frantically. "I'll book a flight and—"

"I'm afraid that's not possible, Mr. Parker."

"Why not? I have to go to her. I have to help—"

"We need you to hang around and answer some questions, sir."

Something in the man's tone wrenched James from his feverish planning. "Hang around?"

"If the bloodstains match your wife's type, the FBI will be called in, and we're working with the authorities in Idaho right now. There is no point in you going up there."

"Are you saying I can't go? Will you keep me from leaving?"

"I don't think it will come to that, sir."

"Are you—" He couldn't wrap his mind around the notion slowly stirring. "I love my wife. She's everything to me. Are you implying that I'm somehow involved in this? Am I a—" He could barely voice the word. "A suspect?"

The man's eyes remained carefully blank. "If you could just answer some questions, Mr. Parker, that would be very helpful."

"You answer me first. You cannot seriously imagine—"

"I try to avoid imagination. In my job, the facts are all that matter. Now, do you know your wife's blood type? And would you happen to have a hairbrush of hers, for DNA matching?"

"On cop shows, they say those closest are always prime suspects when there's foul play." Foul play. Oh, God. Bella…bleeding. Hurt. "This can't be happening." No matter how worried he'd been before, nothing compared with how terrified he was now. Abruptly, he had to sit down. "Bella…" His head sagged into his hands.

"That's television, Mr. Parker. Take a minute to clear your mind."

James raised haunted eyes to the man who sat across from him. "I'd hoped that she was just still mad at me. I never truly believed—" He couldn't finish.

"You had a fight?" Detective Gordon's gaze sharpened. "What about?"

"I should be calling a lawyer, shouldn't I?"

Gordon shrugged. "Your decision. No one's charging you with anything yet."

"Yet." James uttered a rusty chuckle. He sank into the cushions. "Unbelievable."

Then the image hit him again, of Bella hurt. Bleeding. "I'm not going to waste any time with a lawyer. My wife is out there, possibly injured or—" He shook his head violently. "No. She has to be all right. She has to be." He stared at the man before him. "To hell with what the implications are for me. She's been gone for two and a half weeks, and you people are finally paying attention." He stood. "Her blood type is B positive. Her hairbrush is gone, but I'll look around. The housekeeper is here twice a week, so I don't know—what else could serve the same purpose?"

He whirled to race up the stairs, but Gordon's hand on his arm halted him.

"If you wouldn't mind, Mr. Parker, we can do the search."

"But—" Once again, comprehension arose. "Right. You haven't charged me, but that doesn't mean you trust me."

"Can't afford to just yet, sir. So, are you giving us permission to search your house?"

This was a nightmare. But what did he know about criminal lawyers? He was innocent, and meanwhile, the clock was ticking. If there was a chance in the world that Bella could be found...

He swallowed hard. She had to be. He could not

live with the knowledge that their last words had been spoken in anger and despair.

"Yes," he said. "You have my permission." Then a thought occurred. "She hasn't been in my car lately, but we always joked about how she left hairs everywhere—long, black curly—"

Fear robbed him of voice. He hardly registered Gordon's instructions to the officer, words about bringing in a forensics team. After a moment, he regained possession of himself and faced the detective. "My car is in the garage, unlocked."

"Thank you." Gordon paused. "If you have a photograph of your wife, that would be helpful."

"Of course." James crossed the room, retrieved a photo album from the shelves. Halted as fear jolted through him. *Please. Let her be safe. Even if she doesn't want me, her children need her.*

I need her, too. For a second, he was overcome by a longing for her, for the life with her he'd loved so much—a yearning so visceral and sharp it flayed him to the bone.

"Mr. Parker?"

James squeezed his eyes to shut out the vision of the wasteland he would inhabit if Bella were taken from him. Then with painful slowness, he opened the book.

The very first page nearly undid him. Bella, soaking wet, dancing in the mud with a young Cele and toddler Cameron.

He held out the album with shaking hands. "Study

this and tell me I could ever have any desire to kill my wife." He shoved it at the detective. "I was stupid, all right? I lost sight of what was important. Bella and I— God, we were everything to each other, and then somehow…I don't know what the hell happened, but I screwed up, big-time, and Bella went away to think. That's all—she just wanted some time to decide if—" His voice cracked, and he stopped, but he didn't care anymore if he was embarrassing himself. "You've got to find her. I have to tell her I remember everything. That I'm a jerk, and I deserve to be punished, but not by—" He was afraid to say the words, in case doing so gave them power to make his fears come true.

Then he faced the impassive cop before him, forcing eye contact. "I love my wife, Detective. She is everything to me."

The policeman turned away. Pulled out his cell phone.

"Detective—"

Gordon halted.

"What do I tell my children? My son is expecting me to call back."

"How old are they?"

"Twenty-three and nineteen."

"For my money, the truth is always the best place to start, sir."

"So, what is the truth? Is their father a suspect in their mother's disappearance? Is their mother still—" He faltered on the word. "Alive?" He held up a hand.

"She has to be. I'd know it if she wasn't. I'd—" He tapped his heart. "I'd feel it, in here."

Gordon's smile was all pity. "People often think that."

"I'm certain of it."

"I hope you're right, Mr. Parker. Honestly, I do."

"So what about the first question? Am I under suspicion?"

"Everyone's under suspicion in the beginning, sir. It's my job to weed that number down."

"Are you good at your job, Detective?"

"I am."

"I damn sure hope so. That woman is my world."

"Understood." Grim-faced, Gordon flipped open his phone and left the room.

CHAPTER EIGHT

AFTER A SLEEPLESS night, James was in the kitchen, eyes pinned on the coffeepot, wondering how he would make it through the day. Cele was upstairs asleep in her old room, while he'd barely convinced Cameron not to cut classes today.

Not that he didn't understand the instinct to circle the wagons, to huddle together in a vigil after last night's shocking news from Detective Gordon. But there was no telling when the police would find out anything more.

Bella. Dear God, Bella. Every time he'd closed his eyes, terrifying images of her possible fate seared his eyeballs.

He'd focused, instead, on putting the house in order as best he could after the police had left. To their credit, the search had been less invasive than he supposed it could have been.

But he felt violated. The nest Bella had created, the house that had been their sanctuary, had been breached by strangers. He didn't know how to make things feel safe again.

Suddenly, footsteps pounded on the stairs. "Daddy, did you catch the news this morning?" Cele burst into the kitchen. "Quick, turn on the TV." She switched on the little set Bella had sometimes tuned in while she was cooking.

"What's going on?" he asked. "Is there something—"

Cele frantically punched buttons on the remote. "Look—they're showing Mama's picture. Someone sent it to CNN."

James moved toward the television set as if in a dream. "Bella," he murmured, and held out his hand as if he could touch her. "Oh, baby, what happened to you?"

Just then, the telephone rang. James kept his eyes on the screen as he answered it. "Hello?"

"Mr. Parker, it's Detective Gordon. Your wife's been found."

"I'm watching her picture on the screen. I've never seen this photo before. Where is she?" he asked Gordon.

"Colorado."

"Colorado?" he echoed. "Where?"

The detective's voice was grim. "No one knows."

"What do you mean?"

"We're checking on it now. The situation is… unusual."

"But she's alive, right? Is she okay?"

"At this point, Mr. Parker, you know as much as I

do. I'll get back to you when I have more." Then the man was gone, leaving James with an empty phone.

And too many questions.

But one course of action he could definitely pursue. "I'm calling your brother," he said as he gathered a trembling Cele into his arms.

THREE HOURS AFTER Bella's picture had appeared on CNN, James stood in the kitchen that once was the heart of their home, willing the telephone to ring. Palms spread on the tile counter Bella had insisted on learning to lay herself, he curled his fingers, one by one.

"Dad?" His son, Cameron, appeared in the doorway, lanky and as tall as James himself. His mixed-race heritage, African-American and Vietnamese, proclaimed itself in the slant of his near-black eyes, the caramel skin. "Have you talked to Mom yet? Is she okay?"

How could he have for one moment believed that you could love an adopted child less than one of your flesh? Cam was attempting to be cool and grown-up, but vulnerability shadowed every line of his frame. His mother, no matter that they shared no genes— his mother was gone, and he needed her here, every bit as much as his diminutive sister, jiggling an impatient foot, did.

Just as James himself. "I'm waiting for a call back."

Cele leaped to her feet, all coiled fury. "The man who sent in the photo to CNN won't tell anyone where she is," she said to her brother.

Cam went soldier straight. "Has he kidnapped her?" He glanced around. "Where are the cops? Shouldn't the FBI be here?" His outrage and confusion were palpable.

"Slow down, both of you." His father-as-commander voice, the one he hadn't had much use for since Cam graduated from high school. "She's definitely in Colorado, and Detective Gordon connected me with the local sheriff, who says she's perfectly safe, that he's been trying to find out her identity from the beginning, and this is merely a precaution to weed out the kooks. We have to be patient." The lecture was as much for himself as for them.

"We're her family. She doesn't have to be protected from us."

"Yeah," Cele said grimly. "Something's wrong, isn't it?" For a second, his eldest was a scared kid.

James swung between his own fury and desperation, between the craving to be alone before he put a fist through a wall and the responsibility he hadn't been required to wield much lately, to take care of his children.

The father won, if barely. "The sheriff says the man is her doctor and that he needs to talk to me first."

"Why?" Cele was up and pacing again. "What's wrong?"

The phone sounded unnaturally loud. Cam leaped for it, clutched it for a second as though he might answer, then handed it to James.

James hit the talk button and only just resisted the

urge to move somewhere private. "James Parker," he answered.

"This is Dr. Sam Lincoln. Jane is safe," an even baritone voice said.

Jane. "That's not her name."

"I know—sorry. I'm used to calling her that. The sheriff did tell me, though, that her name is Isabella."

"Why didn't she tell you herself? What's wrong? Let me talk to her."

"Not until I'm satisfied that you're really her husband. That you won't harm her."

"Harm her? Are you serious? You have no authority to keep my wife from me."

"Calm down, Mr. Parker. You don't understand what's going on."

"Then you start explaining."

"Mr. Parker, I understand your anxiety, so I'll overlook your attitude. For now."

This man was the key to finding her, so however much his proprietary tone grated on him, James had to get a grip on himself. "What can you tell me about her condition?" Cam and Cele both moved closer.

"She was found on the side of a road, bleeding and unconscious. She had no identification with her."

"But she's conscious now?"

"Yes. And healing well, for the most part."

"I need to see her. Our children do, as well."

"So you have children. Any of them with dark hair?"

"Our son. Why?" He could feel Cam and Cele's frustration at hearing only one side of the conversation.

"Are they adopted?"

"What does it matter? And why haven't you asked Bella that? You said she came out of a coma." He heard Cele's gasp.

"She did. And I apologize. I'm new at this screener duty." Dr. Lincoln paused. "Her physical condition is improving every day. She's pretty much back to normal except for some lingering soreness."

"But?"

"She has retrograde amnesia."

"Amnesia." Beside him erupted questions. He held up one hand for silence as he struggled to absorb the idea. She hadn't called or returned home because she couldn't. His shoulders sagged in relief. "Explain that, exactly."

"Your wife, if she is your wife, emerged from the coma with no memory of her past."

"She's mine. I can prove it. Do you have e-mail?"

"No. Tell me something that isn't in the photo I took."

James thought hard. She had a birthmark her children didn't know about. She wasn't a prude, but he wasn't sure she would be comfortable with them present as he described it. "She has funny second toes. Longer than the big toe."

"Lots of people do."

"She's five foot nine. Curvy." Voluptuous, really, but he was uncomfortable talking about her figure with this man. "Her voice is sexy as hell." Cele's eyes popped wide, and Cam's worried expression eased into a grin.

"Any birthmarks?"

You bastard. "Kids, go in the other room. Just for a minute." They grudgingly complied. "You know she does, and I hate like hell that you've looked."

"I'm her doctor. It's no big deal." But something in his tone had James on edge. "Tell me where it is."

"I would like nothing more than to clean your clock right now."

Lincoln chuckled. "She's a hell of a woman. I don't blame you."

James tried to relax, but the Twenty Questions was killing him. "On the inside of her right thigh." And he'd kissed it a million times.

"Thank you. The sheriff says he's gotten confirmation, but I just want to be very careful. Would you answer me one question? Where do you live?"

"In Parker's Ridge, Alabama."

"The Southern drawl." Lincoln paused. "Here's the deal. We don't know what happened to her because she has no memory of anything before she woke up in the hospital."

"She doesn't even recall her family?"

"Nothing at all until night before last, when she had a sudden image of a baby with dark hair in her arms and a man's hand stroking them both."

The kids peered around the door, and he waved them in, glancing at Cameron, whom they'd adopted as an infant. Cele had been nearly two when they'd found her. "Our son." But James was more impatient than ever. "Why can't I talk to her?"

"Mr. Parker, you have to be patient. I'm her doctor, and her welfare is my only concern."

"She ought to have her family with her."

"Unfortunately, that's not always the case."

"What?" James was outraged. "You are out of your mind. I'll track down this number and be there before—"

"Whoa, there." Another chuckle. "It's been said I have a great bedside manner, but you and I might want to start over. Hear me out, please."

"This better be good."

A long sigh. "The thing with retrograde amnesia is that pressure doesn't help. Expectations can do more harm than good. So if you and your children showed up and she didn't recognize you, it would be traumatic for her and you both, plus it could set back her recovery."

"But it could trigger her memory."

"Maybe. You can't be too careful, however. Especially with someone who wants to remember as badly as she does."

This was killing him. How did he know the guy was even competent? "Explain your credentials."

"I was on the staff of Johns Hopkins for six years, board certified in cardiology. Much of what I'm telling you I've researched with friends—neurologists and psychiatrists—who are still there."

"Your hospital doesn't have them?"

"I wish. Someday, I will."

"But she's in your facility?"

"No. We took her to Denver for an MRI, and there's no permanent brain damage except for the amnesia. Once she regained consciousness, the specialist released her back into my care."

"So where is she staying?"

"I'll tell you, but first we have to figure out the best way to handle this for her sake. You can't just barge in on her."

Everything in him quivered to do exactly that. "Hand her the phone."

"She's not here. She has no idea you called."

James's fingers clenched. "You are making me crazy. I want to be with my wife. Our children need her."

"I can understand how she would inspire such passion," Lincoln said quietly. "But if you love her that much, you want to do what's best for her." He exhaled strongly. "Look, all I'm asking is that you approach this situation with caution. Come, but don't tell her who you are at first. Find out if she recognizes you. It's possible that all the pieces will come together right then, but—"

"But?"

"But if they don't, it will be hard on all of you. You'll expect her to react to you the way you're used to, and she'll sense that. She's a sensitive and giving person. To fail you will cause her pain, and she's already been through a lot." He paused. "The sheriff told me about her car being found. We knew she'd been injured, but we weren't sure how."

"Did they hurt her? Hit her?" James heard his voice going low and brutal. If they'd violated her...

"She's fine now, I promise. She had some lacerations and some bruising, but she was otherwise not injured except for the head trauma."

James closed his eyes in relief. He'd stand beside her even if she had been raped, but he could hardly bear to think of his Bella suffering through that sort of trauma.

"It's highly likely," the doctor continued, "that she will never remember the attack, and we can serve her best by not focusing on it, either." After a moment, he spoke again. "Just these couple of weeks of knowing her, I completely understand how you'd like to tear those guys apart. I'm supposed to do no harm, but I'd gladly help you. She's a remarkable woman."

"My woman."

"I got that. Can't say that I like it, but such is life."

James felt about seventeen and trying to stake out his territory. But he couldn't help himself. Every nerve ending was on fire with his need to get to Bella, to shield her. To make everything all right. "What are the chances—" he forced himself to confront the unbearable "—that she'll ever remember us?"

"Pretty good. If you allow her time and don't force the issue."

So that was the nub of it—if he truly wished the best for Bella, he had to fight his natural urges. "I want to be there, however this must be done."

"If the kids can handle the situation and back off if needed, I think you all should make the trip. There's a little café in town, nothing much, but the food's good and filling. When I know you've arrived, I'll bring her over for a meal. If the sight of you jogs her memory, all to the good."

"And if not?"

"Then we go to plan B. I don't know what that is yet. I'll call my sources and have some suggestions for you by the time you get here."

"Where exactly are you?" Mentally, he was already on a plane.

"Lucky Draw, Colorado. Nearly to Utah."

"Never heard of it." What on earth was she doing that far away? Had she really been planning to leave him?

"Few have. We're not a ski resort. This is hard country. Old mining towns. Folks who have to fight to survive."

"I'll find it."

They spent a few moments discussing logistics in a calmer fashion, then the doctor chuckled. "You call her Bella?"

"I do," James said. "It's my name for her." *Only mine.* "Why?"

"I was just thinking that my housekeeper will get a kick out of knowing that. She's Italian, and she kept calling her *bella,* which is Italian for beautiful. It seemed apt, and for a while I wondered if that might be a solution when Jane was auditioning names."

James found himself smiling. Only Bella, the

woman who saw the world differently from anyone he'd ever met, would insist on giving names a trial run.

Then the man's words sank in. "Your housekeeper? Where is Bella staying?"

"With me."

"Why?"

"She had nowhere to go, Mr. Parker. No money, no family."

Every word was a nail in his heart. To think of Bella so alone, hurt and afraid.

"She's staying in the garage apartment, if that makes you feel any better."

"Nothing will make me feel better until I can be with her. Bring her back home."

"That may not happen soon, Mr. Parker. Please understand that."

He didn't want to. Everything in James longed to race to her side, hold her tight and steal her away. Watch over her every second and make sure she never suffered again.

She was so far away from him. Mentally and physically. Disheartened, James finished the conversation and hung up, but he was reluctant to release the receiver, his only link to the woman he'd loved most of his life.

He drew himself straight and turned to his children, reminding himself that they were adults, and he didn't have to sugarcoat anything.

"Your mom doesn't know she has a family," he began. "But let's get packed and go remind her that there are people who love her very much."

CHAPTER NINE

"HOW FAR IS IT to his house?" Cele asked as she paced the dining area of Lucky Draw's lone café.

James stood at the window, staring outside. Wishing that he'd been unfair and asked the kids to stay home until he'd had a chance to test the waters.

What if she remembered why she'd left? Blurted out something in front of Cele and Cam? Not that he didn't deserve the humiliation. But he wanted a chance to explain.

You tried that already and look what happened.

He'd never been this nervous, not the first night they'd made love, not before their wedding.

"Daddy?"

James steeled himself not to bark at her. They were all worried. "What did you ask?"

"I said—"

Just then, Cam snapped to attention. A smile, that goofy one Bella loved, spread over his features. "Mom. It's Mom—" He sprang into motion.

"Cam, don't." Though James understood the impulse.

Cameron's shoulders sank. "Yeah. I know, I just—"

"Mama," Cele whispered, and approached her brother's side, blocking James's view.

He caught only the merest glimpse of curly hair before Bella passed out of sight.

But his heart knew.

Thank God. Oh, thank God. He closed his eyes. *She's here. She's safe. Everything else can be worked out.*

A tiny sound from his daughter had him reaching for her, but he could focus on nothing else but the woman walking through the doorway.

Bella. Oh, my love.

The best part was that this was the Bella he'd loved so fiercely, her jeans dirty, her hair windblown. A smile was blooming up out of him. Bella the gardener, the digging-in-the-dirt-makes-me-happy woman who'd made his life a roller-coaster ride of unexpected and offbeat pleasures.

His feet began to move, and his heart raced. "Bella—" Despite his cautions to the kids, he longed to grab her, swing her around as he had so many times. To kiss her until neither of them could breathe, to make love to her for hours—

A small, strangled sound from Cele brought him up short.

And he saw what he should have noticed first thing.

Bella wasn't smiling.

She was scared. Of them. The family she had once adored.

He glanced at the man beside her.

The man shook his head, pity in his eyes.

THE THREE PEOPLE were staring at her so hard that Jane skidded to a stop. Were they her family? The way they zeroed in on her, the tiny blonde with tears on her cheeks, the lanky boy with his heart in his eyes…

Nothing. Not a thing seemed familiar about any of them.

A man stood behind them, tall and strong and handsome, his blue gaze locked on hers as the smile on his face faded.

"I—" She glanced at Sam and knew it was true.

He squeezed her shoulder. "It's okay."

She shook her head. "No, it isn't." Looked back at them. "I—I'm sorry." Her voice was a croak, her throat tight with disappointment. "I should—" she switched from one to the next, wishing for something, anything "—I really wanted—"

They were gazing at her with such hope, so much longing. She couldn't breathe. Had to get away before—

"Forgive me," she managed to say. She tore her gaze from them, began backing toward the door.

"Jane," Sam said. "It's okay."

But panic had her and wouldn't let go. "It's not. I—I thought—" She whirled and ran.

Behind her, she heard voices, pleading. Arguing.

She hurried around to the back, desperate to be alone, to think, to breathe.

"Bella." Not Sam now, she understood. *Him.* Her…husband.

She didn't turn around. "Why do you call me that?"

"Bella? It's my name for you. Your full name is Isabella Rosaline Parker. Your maiden name was Grant. But from the beginning, I called you Bella."

She recalled that second of hesitation when Luisa had first used the term *bella.* This man must be telling the truth, but—

"I don't…know your name." A bitter laugh was startled from her. Furiously, she swiped at the tears. "I'm sorry."

"Don't be. It's James. James Cameron Parker." So kind, his voice, but layered with more. Disappointment. Determination. Some other current she couldn't really name.

She heard his footsteps and cringed. Faced him.

Pain shadowed his features. She'd married this handsome, well-dressed man? She frowned down at her clothes.

He smiled, a beautiful one. "I've seen you like this a thousand times."

"Like…this?"

He nodded. "You had the most beautiful gardens in town, and you did all the work yourself."

But one word had caught her. "Had?"

He hesitated. "You've been…busy lately."

There was a lot of misery in that statement. The

weight of questions she needed to ask and fears she was afraid to voice crowded her chest.

Sometimes important people from the past can do more harm than good, Sam had warned her.

"Why?" Then she shook her head. "No, forget that." She struggled for one deep breath. "The children. They're...ours?"

"Yes. Cele is twenty-three. Cameron is nineteen."

"Sam told me I hadn't borne a child."

His eyes went dark. "You had miscarriages."

Plural. She'd lost more than one baby. Her mind went to that dark head.

"So we adopted them. Cele was nearly two. Cam was an infant."

"The memory," she murmured. "A baby."

"You're remembering things?"

She lifted one shoulder. "Only that one, except for an image of some blue flower—"

"Plumbago. One of your favorites."

Her hand fluttered. "There's so much." Her throat was tight, her head spinning. "I—I don't know where to start." Her heart was flopping inside her chest, and her vision was darkening.

"Hey—" Suddenly, he was there, this James, this man she didn't know. He scooped her up as though she weighed nothing, but she was frightened of the awful feeling in her head and her chest.

"Bella, breathe, baby. Come on, easy now—"

"Sam," she barely managed to say. "I need Sam." She attempted to scramble away, but she was so dizzy.

"Put her down." Sam's voice. Safety.

The man's grip tightened. "I didn't hurt her. She just—"

But his hold was so confining, and she was struggling, crying out, "Sam—"

Blue eyes, anguished.

"Please," she gasped. "Please let me go."

He released her abruptly.

And Sam drew her close. She buried her face in his shoulder and trembled.

"I think you'd better go now," Sam said.

"The hell I will," the man James replied. Her husband. How could she not remember him? Her children, but they were no longer babies. She'd hurt them, hurt him.

Hurt, hurt, only hurt...

The darkness won.

CELE, THEIR TOUGH little Cele, was sobbing in her brother's arms.

His tough little Cele, perhaps he should say. Bella hadn't recognized her any more than him or Cam.

And he'd caused all of this, every bit of the pain. He was the one who'd faltered. Who'd forgotten Bella, the real Bella, long before she'd forgotten him. The pain was crushing. For a second, he wondered if he might be having a heart attack his chest ached so fiercely.

How did it feel when a heart died? If he never got Bella back, he might as well—

Cut the crap. You're all those kids have now. And you're used to shouldering heavy loads.

He opened his arms to one heartbroken young woman and a boy trying very hard to be a man. "Come here," he urged. He caught them close, both of them, though Cam hadn't accepted a hug in years. He'd been a good dad, he thought, but Bella had been the nurturer, the one to dry tears and talk out broken hearts.

Sorry, kids, but you're stuck with me. For now, he corrected. Bella would remember. She had to.

Agony roasted his insides as he recalled the terror on Bella's face. Never once in their lives together had she feared him. Had any reason to.

And she'd called for that son of a—

Ruthlessly, James made himself relax. The poisoned barb was still there, but he'd survived tough times before, tougher than this.

No, not tougher. He'd had Bella then.

He embraced his children. Lowered his head to theirs. "We knew this could happen," he began. "But it's going to be okay, I swear it."

Cele looked up with tear-stained cheeks. "Will it, Daddy? How can she not remember us? We're her children. She loves us—"

They were grown now, but they wanted his reassurance, however rocky he felt on the inside. "She does love you," he said firmly. "This is simply a medical problem, and she's just not well yet. But she will be."

"You can't promise that." Cameron's face revealed his yearning to be wrong.

"Your mother will get better." She had to. "She's a very strong woman, and you are her world."

"You are, Daddy, more than us. Everyone knows how in love you two are."

Please make it true. That years of devotion will win in the end. "Children are special," he said. "We've got all sorts of weapons in our armory."

"Like what?" Cam was obviously shaken by the events.

I understand completely, son. Never in my life would I have imagined Bella shrinking from my touch.

He exhaled as he cast his thoughts about. "I hesitate to call this a war…more like a campaign…." His eyebrows rose. "That's it, exactly. Hearts and minds."

"What do you mean?"

He smiled, more out of hope than assurance. "There's a saying about conducting a war by setting out to win over the population rather than by fighting on the battlefield." He chuckled at their perplexed expressions. "We don't push to make your mother remember us."

"What?"

"Nope," he said, warming to the notion. Any plan was better than the misery of inaction. "We hang around for a while. Make ourselves useful. Let Bella get to know us instead of pressuring her to remember. She loved us once." He glanced from one to the other. "Why not fall for us all over again?"

"But what if—" Cele had always been his worrier.

"No, Dad's right. It's a brilliant plan." Cam grinned. "What's not to love about us?"

The ego of youth, James mused. The certainty they'd bred in their children, the understanding that they were fully loved. He drew heart from the notion, and did not doubt that Bella would indeed find herself adoring the children she'd formed.

Him, though—would the man attract her as much as the cocky boy had? Who was he now, and who was she? Had they stayed together out of habit, or was there still something special between them?

He was flat scared, to be honest. When had the magic left? Could they get it back?

Once it had been powerful, all-consuming.

He would make her love him again.

And when she remembers that you blew it?

For a second, James had a moment of uncharacteristic indecision. If he could make Bella fall in love with him once more, would that love survive, should she recall the end?

No time to weaken; his kids were depending on him for answers. "Let's get some lunch. We have plans to make." He would keep himself too busy to think about how it had felt to have the one love of his life run into the arms of another man.

JANE LAY in the cool, dim room that had seemed so strange once, now a refuge she sought as eagerly as a man's embrace.

She pressed her lips together so the moan

wouldn't escape, but she couldn't still the heart that insisted on racing despite her every effort at calm.

She had run to Sam. Not to *him*, that man. Husband by law but not in her heart. She'd hurt him badly, she could tell. He'd swept her up simply in a move to protect.

But he'd wanted so much from her, more than she could bear to feel.

She was breathing too fast. She tightened her fingers on the bedspread and pondered the yellowed ceiling above. The one little stain her own personal Rorschach test. Focused on its margins, brown fading to yellow, then cream, in no design she could discern.

The bulbs. Think on them, on the gardening you will do tomorrow. Irises, big Dutch ones, purple as night's deepest shadows. The buttery streak down each throat.

Her breathing steadied, as did her pulse. She had refused the sedative Sam had prescribed. She'd wanted his comfort, yes, but not his pills. Needed the safe harbor he represented, when her mind had short-circuited after the emotional overload.

That was how Sam had explained it, the dizziness, the near faint. Exactly what he'd worried about, and what she'd demanded, this chance to connect with her past.

But she hadn't really believed him. How could one not recognize those one held most dear? Wouldn't their presence get a messenger past the barriers thrown up by her body in the wake of injury? She'd been so certain that the walls were only a papery shell, easily punctured by the arrow that was true love.

Yet the reinforcements had held, despite the siege of a family armed with love and longing even a stranger could feel.

Stranger. Her last hope crumbled. She was an enigma to everyone, even herself. She sat up suddenly, seeking a stronger posture than cowering flat on her back. She wasn't yet up to standing, and the desire for a shield had her drawing her knees to her chest, curling her arms around them to protect the frightened creature within.

She wasn't taking this lying down, damn it.

Gripping her forearms, she turned her head to the side, relieved to see that night had not yet fallen. The day that had begun with so much promise, if such nerves, was not over.

She wasn't ready to talk to him, the man named James. But she could at least manage a visit with the children.

She lifted an image of each one from the tumble of emotions, the diminutive woman who had looked at her with a girl's nerves—and a woman's challenge. That one, her daughter—her *daughter*—would be a tough nut to crack, she thought. She might want her mother, but she would fight for the father she so obviously adored.

The boy would be easier, less threatening. He stood a head taller than his sister, but he was still caught between man and boy and vulnerable in the way that young males are, not yet grown into their longer bones, posturing to frighten off the monsters while still wishing someone else would make them go away.

He was beautiful in his own manner, with dark eyes you wanted to sink right into and melt. Stick-straight black hair…her fingers flexed as if to curve around an earlier, smaller version of that head.

You had miscarriages. Sorrow there. She placed one palm over her womb. *So we adopted.*

Her mind flashed to the hands that had held her tight.

This James Parker owned the hand in her memory. Her drawing. She was almost certain of that, however overcome she'd been at the time. Nonetheless, she scrambled from the bed and made her way to where the simple drawing lay on the tiny kitchen table.

Oh, yes. Her mind flicked back and forth, dream to drawing to sketchy memory only hours old.

That hand. His hand. Cradling both her and the baby close.

But though she could connect the dots, she couldn't connect the emotions. She stood outside herself, an observer only.

The lines of fingers and palms might be the same. Obviously, even through her tumult, she'd recognized that the man James had powerful feelings for both his children and her.

But she only felt pity and shame right now. And fear.

Not of them, perhaps, but of whatever world they'd drag her into, for that was how things seemed right now. She could accept their claims and go with them, but she wouldn't be returning home, as they would.

She would be leaving home, however recent and tenuous, behind.

She wasn't ready.

Oh, God, after all that yearning…she could not go.

JAMES KICKED a dirt clod as he walked around this odd hamlet time had forgotten. He'd visited many small towns, of course, in his part of Alabama, the northeast corner filled with what natives called mountains but people here would likely dismiss as mere bumps.

The café was the newest structure, and it had surely been built in the 1940s. There was a squat brick building that housed a small grocery with a minuscule post office, and an old-style gas station with two pumps beneath a tin canopy, run by perhaps the oldest man James had ever seen. Houses more like cabins were sprinkled here and there, but James was headed for one tucked back on a road at the edge of town. Their waitress had told them Dr. Sam lived there.

Dr. Sam. His nemesis. Bella's savior.

His prelunch resolve was strained. He'd always been a patient man; Bella was the one who chafed at waiting. He could handle whatever time was required, be it for negotiations with a supplier or for making sweet love to his wife.

But he'd found her when he'd feared her dead. Gotten the scent of her in his nostrils, the feel of her on his skin. Another man was standing between him and her, and most of what was civilized in James had vaporized under the glare of his drive to stake his claim. Bella was his, damn it. Whether she knew it or not.

He'd been counting on memory to carry the day, to bridge the gap that his mistake had set in motion.

Dread that he alone would not be enough to win her sent a cold line of sweat down his back. He stopped at the base of the road climbing up to where she stayed. Inspected the surroundings with a hunter's eye.

He was on foot with no weapons but his brain. In the past, that would have been enough, in his real life, all he'd needed.

But here and now…he was all but naked. Defenseless. He understood far too little of his enemy, of Bella's mind-set, her condition. All signs pointed to the demand to take things slow.

If only his insides would agree.

James had never been to war, but he'd read a lot of military history. You didn't win a skirmish or a battle, much less a war, by jumping the gun. You performed surveillance, you readied your troops, you made certain you were well provisioned.

There were a million details he should be dealing with back home, a business on the brink, a staggering load of responsibilities.

He cared for none of them, not one whit.

But if he was to bring Bella back, he could not let their home lie unprotected. He had to find some means to deal with what he must from here....

Because he was not leaving Lucky Draw without her.

Cele was back in town, on the phone to the plant. She was eager and capable, ready to assume some of the load. He would let her.

Cameron must return to school, but he could help, too. He was a solid pilot, and James would put that skill to use. Cam could fly Cele back and forth this astonishing distance. He could ferry what was required for James to do business the old way, with paper documents, since James sincerely doubted that Lucky Draw had Wi-Fi or hi-speed cable. FedEx.

All that pressed in on James made him tired, but he would manage. He always had. For now, though, he would do reconnaissance on the enemy's lair, figure out where the princess was being held.

James had to grin—that sounded much more like a Bella fancy—at least, the Bella of the old days.

His ire was up; his juices were running. James hadn't had a challenge like this in a very long time, and he was surprised at how it energized him.

First step, survey the battlefield.

Step two, shamelessly use your children as bait.

Bella would have laughed, the old Bella, the daredevil. He had no idea who this woman, this memory-less Bella was.

Please, he prayed. *Please let me have my Bella back.*

Then he began to plot. A quarterback was the general of the playing field, and he'd been a good one.

He'd conduct this campaign with all the weapons at his disposal, every understanding of Bella's nature he possessed. He'd tempt her unmercifully with what he'd learned during their rich, beautiful life together, and he'd adapt to the changed circumstances.

This Bella was not the girl he'd married or the woman with whom he'd spent thirty-six years, though time would tell how much of either slept inside her.

He'd turn the tables on her, make her love him again. He'd fallen like a ton of bricks years ago, while she'd played hard to get.

James smiled. Maybe the gambit to begin was a little *hard-to-get* of his own.

Even if it killed him.

Which it just might.

But he'd always liked a challenge. And he'd never met one quite like Bella, past or present.

CHAPTER TEN

"BELLA," LUISA CALLED from outside her door. "You have a visitor."

Bella. Jane tensed. She should be changing her name, but she wasn't ready yet.

"A handsome young man, that one. A little shy, I think."

"Luisa, I can't."

"Can't what?" The doorknob rattled. Began to turn. "Cannot spare a moment for someone who has done nothing to hurt you? He only asks for a moment."

"But—" Jane closed her eyes. Swallowed. Luisa was right. The boy had done nothing to her. None of them had.

Then Luisa stood there in the afternoon's golden light. "He tells me, this one, with his pretty manners, that he understands that you do not recognize him. That he must return to college and he would simply like a moment to be with you, after all the worry they have been through."

To refuse would be churlish. Cowardly. "Do you think I was a weak woman…before?"

"Oh, no. You are passion. Life. One does not seize the reins as you have if one is accustomed to being cosseted."

"How can you say that?" But Jane grinned. "And don't give me that palmistry nonsense again."

"Very well." Luisa sniffed. "I know what I know. Now, where will you meet with him, this Cameron?"

Jane glanced around her but felt the call of the sun. "Outside. In the garden."

"Or what will one day be a garden, if Dr. Sam does not undo all your hard work?"

A chill ran through her. Luisa assumed she would leave with them, these strangers. Go...home. The one she didn't remember.

Jane halted, then forced herself to continue.

Hoping that something, someone, would prove to be the key that would open the lock. Once in the garden, she glanced around for her visitor, but not seeing him, sank to her knees and began weeding to still her nerves.

"Mom? Uh, I mean, um—I don't—"

Grasping a weed, she settled back on her heels. Turned to find him towering over her, shifting on his feet.

"I'm sorry." He held out his palms. "I don't mean to make you feel bad. I don't know what to call you."

So earnest. So worried and...young.

He would not hurt her.

She stood. Smiled as she hungrily scanned his features, tried to see the baby in the man. "But I am your mother, right?"

"Yeah." His shoulders relaxed.

"So you should call me that. It's not—" She gestured futilely back toward the village. "That wasn't about me not wanting you. It was just…"

"Too much."

She smiled. "Yes." He could use a hug, she thought, but the one she would offer was not a mother's. Wouldn't that hurt worse? So she fell back on some notion of hospitality she didn't recall learning. "Would you like something to drink?" Then she frowned. "All I have is tea."

"Iced tea would be great."

"I—all I have is herbal tea. I'm sorry. Maybe Luisa would—"

"Herbal tea is just fine." In his firm tone, she glimpsed hints of the man he would become. He pointed behind her. "It's good to see you gardening again."

"He—your father. He said I had big ones. Did all the work."

"Worked harder than any hired hand, Grandpa says."

"Grandpa? My—" Why hadn't she felt it, that she had parents alive?

"No, Dad's dad. Your—" He shuffled his feet. "I don't know what I'm supposed to be telling you."

"Whatever the truth is. I have to start somewhere. Begin as—"

"—you mean to continue," he finished.

Her eyes widened. "Why do you say that?"

"You only repeated it to me and Cele about a

thousand times in our lives. We might as well have it tattooed on our foreheads."

How incredible. Another piece that had made it through the darkness. "But then you'd only notice it in the mirror. I was thinking on the backs of your hands."

His gaze cut to hers, his face lighting up. "You made a joke. I've missed that."

"I joke around? Why did I quit?"

"You've been working long hours since I left home, I think."

"Are you in college?"

"Yes." He nodded. "And flight school, thanks to you."

"Me?"

"Dad was after me to join the business, but Cele's more suited to that. You argued my case better than any lawyer. I mean, he's right that if I'm not in the military I miss out on the best part of flying, but—"

She touched his arm, this good-hearted boy, and both of them faltered. "I'm sorry." She withdrew.

"No. That's not why—" His face crumpled. "I know I'm not supposed to push you, but—" He wiped his arm across his eyes. "I never wanted to hug you so much in my life."

Maybe she didn't recollect their past, but she cared about him already, this boy who might have been the baby she'd dreamed of. Longed for. Bella opened her arms and embraced him.

His head collapsed on her shoulder, and his frame shook.

She swayed side to side, as though he were still a baby. A small tune threaded its way through her, and she began to hum.

His embrace nearly crushed her then. "You sang that to me every night until I got too big."

She reared back. "Really?"

"Yeah." Hope and love and fear tangled in his gaze.

Tense and uncertain, Jane froze for a second, then she touched his cheek and continued singing, her voice gaining strength. She cradled the back of his head and urged him down.

He folded into her, this gangly, sweet boy, and she was prepared to stand there as long as he was willing, soaking up the warmth of love she could feel, even if she couldn't recall it. She mourned for the black hole that separated baby from young man and prayed that someday she would regain it all, everything that had been stolen from her.

When slowly he straightened, he wiped his nose with the back of his hand, and she had the notion that she'd witnessed him doing that more than once. "Here," she said, grasping his hand, drawing him into the apartment. "Let's get you a tissue."

He sniffed. "I'd use my shirttail. It drove you nuts."

Had she ever possessed the luxury of worrying over such foolish things? "Well, now I don't care." She handed him a tissue. "But since Luisa does the laundry, let's cut her a break." She smiled.

When he smiled back, the sun couldn't begin to compete.

"Cele is dying to visit you. Can I bring her?"

"May I." She halted. Blinked.

His grin widened. "You sound like a mom. Mine, to be exact."

She owed him honesty. "Cameron, I shouldn't get your hopes up. I want badly to be the mother you remember, but I'm just winging it right now."

He nodded, but he refused to let her spoil his cheer, this sunny boy she was happy was hers. "I'm a good pilot. Winging it is my life."

She sat down, exhausted from the accumulated emotion. "Do you think that your sister would mind if I took a little nap first? I don't want to hurt her, but I'm just—"

His eyes widened. "I'm sorry. I didn't mean to—I forgot you've been hurt. Here—why don't you get into bed, and I'll just sit here and watch over you while—"

She grabbed his hand. "It's okay." How lovely that the man had raised a boy who was a protector, too. She would have to speak to the man again, as well.

But not yet.

"Come on." As though he were the adult and she the child, Cameron led her to the bed and urged her down, then tenderly covered her with a quilt.

She surrendered to his care. All the starch had gone out of her suddenly. "Don't wait, please. Just need to be…" *Alone,* she thought as she drifted off. She craved some space to heal, to try to understand all that had happened.

But part of her longed to beg him to stay.

"I'M GOING BACK," Cele said as evening approached.

James disconnected his call. "I've got us rooms in Rifle. It's the closest town with a motel, though God knows what kind of accommodations they are."

"No, I mean I'm going home."

James frowned. Her face was set and pale. "You haven't seen your mother yet."

"I've seen enough." He recognized that stubborn set of jaw.

Inwardly, he sighed. They'd been through a lot in Cele's early days. Abandoned as a baby, then left in an orphanage in Romania, she'd been hard to connect with at first, then clingy.

But once Cele understood that she was theirs and vice versa, that she truly belonged, well…look out. She had a mulish streak a mile wide, and it was worse when she was hurt.

His prickly darling required some handling. She and Bella had survived her teens, but just barely. Bella was warm and generous and open, but she had a stubborn streak of her own.

"She'll wake up soon," he promised. "Then you'll be the first one she wants to talk to."

"No," she said quietly. Too quietly. "Cam already was."

Lord save me from mother-daughter dynamics. But he couldn't miss the streak of pain.

"Honey, Cam's easy. He's a goof. If you had to deal with any of us and you were scared, who would you choose?"

"But she doesn't even know Cam," she cried. "She doesn't remember any of us. She has no idea he's easy, and she still picked him." She whirled away, but not before he spotted the too-bright eyes.

It wasn't that he didn't understand. He, too, had felt the sting of Bella's fear. More like a slap, though. A blow, straight to the center of his chest. How could she not sense, deep inside, what they meant to each other? The unbreakable bond?

"Hey," he said quietly, offering up his arms.

She faced him, blinking rapidly. "I hate this." With a delicate sniff, a brush at her eyes. "I just want Mama back."

"Me, too, sweetheart." Once again, he offered, and this time, she accepted the comfort. Clung to him. He rested his head on her hair, though he had to bend low. "You do what you have to, Cele. If this is too much, you can certainly go, and I'll keep you posted." He leaned back. "I'm going to ask you to stand in for me for a while, anyway."

Her head whipped up. "Really?"

"Really."

Her eyes shone. "But—"

"No buts. We'll tag team them, my girl. I trust you, and you're smart as they come. We'll talk every day."

At that moment, she seemed very young to him, and he wondered if he was making a mistake, throwing her to the wolves, even part-time. "You think I'm ready?"

"Others won't, Cele. I'm not telling you it will be easy, but you're ready to make your move. The next generation of Parkers steps up to the plate."

"But what about Mama?"

"Give things another day, won't you? She's been through a lot. I bet tomorrow will be a different story, and she needs all of us. Go to her and explain why you're leaving—don't just run."

Irritation flared, replaced by a smile. "Parkers don't run when things get tough."

He winked. "That's my girl."

"Okay." A big sigh. "All right. So…" She was already planning, he could tell. "I'll get my laptop, and we'll start outlining what has to be done, what I should send to you, the issues that must be addressed—"

James couldn't help his chuckle.

"What?" She turned. But then she smiled, too. "Your busy bee, huh, Daddy?"

He rumpled her hair affectionately. "Parker's Ridge better batten down the hatches. Storm Cele is fixing to make landfall."

She gave him a quick hug, then, in an instant, was out the door.

BUT BELLA DID NOT wake up refreshed. She didn't wake up at all, though that damn Dr. Sam, the self-appointed gatekeeper, said she was fine, only sleeping.

James went over Cele's lists with her. Counseled an uncertain Cam, though he was sure of little himself. They ate one more meal in the diner, lingered for a while, then finally, there was no choice but to go. To put nearly fifty miles between them and the woman they had traveled so far to claim.

As he slouched on the bed in his solitary room, he absently clicked cable channels but registered nothing on the screen. Idly, he cataloged the amenities of the so-called Red Crown Inn, which, he'd been assured, boasted the finest of accommodations for a hundred miles.

The room was huge, in the manner of a bygone day. There was easily space for a second king-size bed beside the one he occupied. The cabbage-rose drapes in hues of salmon and pale green complemented the dark green carpet—and all smelled of someone's heavy hand at floral room spray, which didn't do much to cover the darker scents of forty years or so of cigarettes and mildew and the unique fragrance of time.

The place was less sterile than the usual chain hotel, down-home in its own manner, but altogether miserable.

And he was a snob. Bella had said that, more than once....

"YOU DON'T STRAY OUT of your comfort zone much, do you, rich boy?" Bella, naked, lay on a quilt in a forest clearing where he'd taken her on a hike when he'd brought her home to meet his parents.

He was torn between throwing the edge of the quilt over her, lest someone should happen by, and jumping her bones. Again. And they'd only been there half an hour.

"I do things," he protested.

Mischief sparkled as she popped a grape in her mouth, then slipped it between her lips and into his, slick and slightly warm from her on the outside, chilled when he bit down. "What, besides shock the living daylights out of your parents by showing up with me?"

"They weren't shocked. They were…" He lost his train of thought as she wrapped her fingers around him.

"Don't kid a kidder. They're horrified." She grinned as she slowly squeezed, then trailed her fingers upward. "They're just too mannerly to admit it."

James blinked to clear his brain. She did this, mesmerized him with sex, partly out of fun but also, he was discovering, to afford herself an edge when she felt insecure.

He swept her fingers away and levered himself over her in one swift motion. "I'm the heir. And they're good parents. They only want the best for me." He bent to her then, sliding his tongue down her throat.

A little pleasure hum emerged. "And they're positive that's not me. That I won't fit in here."

He'd already fastened his mouth on her nipple, so he didn't answer immediately. Instead, he concentrated on making certain she felt his devotion. When he'd reduced her to jelly, he lifted his head. "Honey, you fit in everywhere—and nowhere. That's what I love about you—one thing, anyway. You are one of a kind. I'm crazy about you."

It wasn't often that you could catch Bella off guard. Her life, with its revolving relatives, interspersed with months when her mother's craziness would subside, had both toughened her and freed her. Orphaned her and deprived her. Bella had learned to flaunt her uniqueness before others could reject her for it.

But she had the most tender heart he'd ever encountered. Why no one else had discovered that, he could not imagine.

That understanding was his gift to her, along with the one he wanted to give her now, instead of waiting as he'd planned, until they graduated: the knowledge that he would protect that tender heart for the rest of his life. Give it a home, so that she would be rootless no longer.

"You just like how I am in bed," she said. "Some girls mistake great sex for love, but not me."

He barely resisted the urge to don his pants. But that was what she was after, to gain distance. To protect herself. She was a walking contradiction, the wild, free, crazy woman and the starved-for-love girl.

She needed him, he realized. And he wanted to be there for her. Always.

"You're full of it," he said, then charged ahead, though it was not the romantic proposal he'd always assumed he'd make. "Marry me."

Her eyes popped wide. "What?" She scrambled upward. "Are you insane?"

"No. I'm in love with you."

"James, you can't—" she spluttered. "The very idea is absurd."

He might have chosen to be insulted, reacted in knee-jerk hurt, if he hadn't noticed how frightened she was. Yet how she yearned.

He got right in her face. "Double-dog dare you." He was amazed at himself, at how he could be so frivolous, so unconcerned about how correct she was. His family would go berserk.

"It makes no sense." Her voice was almost pleading. "*We* make no sense."

But, in an unusual moment of piercing insight, he recognized how much she wanted to be argued out of her stance.

He could soothe her with sex, but that was her tactic. For the first time in his life, James had no illusions, was not safely blind, cradled in the lovely picture his parents had painted.

To grant them due credit, they were honestly happy—with each other, their lives, the future they anticipated. He admired that. Had thought he wanted that.

Until Bella blew through his life like a blue norther, and rendered his world unfathomable without her.

Honesty was his only angle. "I'm a stick in the mud. You're a butterfly. I won't deny either." He felt ridiculous, kneeling buck naked before her, but intuition told him that they had to slough off both their protective shields. He grasped her hands between his, though in another time, they'd be laughing themselves silly at this Victorian pose.

"Even a butterfly gets tired of floating sometimes." Before she could protest that she wasn't tired or she didn't need rescuing, he bared his own soul. "And an old brown stick should have color in its life, or it's just dying wood."

Moisture shimmered in her gaze. "Oh, James…"

Despite his resolve, he wasn't confident enough to rest his case yet. "I'll go wherever you wish. However far away. You'll wither here, I understand that. I have no desire to change you, not ever. I love exactly who you are."

She was weeping silently now, helplessly, his proud, defiant Bella. "I can't let you give all this up. They adore you, James. That's too big a sacrifice. And I don't want to hurt them."

"We'll work it out, love. All of it. Say yes." He'd abandoned all pride then. "Please. All I need in the world is you."

HE'D BEEN SO CERTAIN of himself, the invincibility of their love, James pondered now. His parents, stunned and grieving, had nonetheless cared for him enough to offer them their blessing. To give Bella a fairy-tale wedding, standing in for the family she'd never had.

They'd ridden off into the sunset, like a couple of celluloid lovers, with about that much depth of understanding of what they faced. There is no certainty like that of young lovers, mesmerized by bountiful sex and full to the brim of all they'll accomplish due to their superior understanding of the world their forebears bobbled.

I don't think I can live this way anymore. Something inside me is dying.

He'd gone back on every last word of it, he realized now. Caged the butterfly who'd had the poor judgment to land on him. He wondered if she'd been so knee-deep in their children and their busy lives that she'd lost sight, too, of how far they'd strayed.

Not that she hadn't agreed with the decisions they'd made. But looking back through the prism of who they'd become and what they'd lost, he began to see how much of their direction she must have concurred with simply because family was everything to her.

He'd betrayed who she was long before he'd broken the vow of fidelity with one moment of carelessness, one terrible, foolish step down the wrong road.

But how did you apologize to a woman who remembered none of it—who she'd been, who he'd been, what he'd encouraged her to become?

He clicked off the television and threw his legs over the side of the mattress, burying his face in his hands. Where did he start, making this up to her, all of it? Did any of that butterfly remain?

He remembered her dirt-stained jeans, the bloom on her face in those initial, carefree minutes before she'd entered the café. The fingers that had once touched him with so much love, shorn of ornamentation now, even the ring he longed to put on her again.

He felt in his pocket for it. He'd discovered it after she'd left and been scared to death by its presence, as though she'd already bid him adieu.

He'd have to earn that right, and the place to begin was by finding out who Bella was now, who she wanted to be. Listening hard and paying attention without the veil of his own desires and needs.

He picked up the phone and ordered a second rental car, paying a premium for the SUV to be delivered first thing in the morning, so Cele and Cam would also have transportation.

Because he couldn't sleep this far away from her, he would drive back to Lucky Draw, and he would park as close as possible to where she lay.

And he would keep watch. For his Sleeping Beauty, whom every cell in him craved to awaken with a kiss.

CHAPTER ELEVEN

JAMES WOKE UP shivering and cursed himself for not thinking to bring a blanket. He sat up in the backseat of the rental car, where he'd retreated when he couldn't keep his eyes open another second.

The backseat was no more comfortable than the front. He rolled his neck to work out the kinks and turned to the right—

And nearly jolted out of his skin.

An old woman stood there, glaring at him. She was barely taller than Cele, bundled into a coat he couldn't help envying, warm and thick, bright red wool.

"You go," she ordered. "Or I will call the police." Her frown far outstripped her size.

"There are no police." Had there been, perhaps Bella would have been restored to him sooner.

"We have a sheriff."

"Whose office is forty-five miles as the crow flies. I've talked to him."

Then her eyes widened. "You are *him*." The word was not a compliment. "The one who claims he is her husband."

He was sick of talking through the glass. He pulled the door handle and pushed gently to move her back.

She didn't budge willingly, but she did go.

He rose to his full height. Later, he might find this amusing, that he felt the need to intimidate someone a good foot shorter. "I *am* her husband."

A disbelieving sniff. "Dr. Sam is unhappy with you."

"Well, I'm pretty unhappy with Dr. Sam myself. He has no authority over Bella or me."

"He saved her life."

Point to Dr. Sam. Blast it. "And I'm grateful for that, I am—but I'm ready to take her home now. To familiar things. People she knows. The home she loves." If only he hadn't witnessed how terrified she'd been by what should have been most familiar, namely him and the kids.

"She is comfortable here. We have cared for her very well."

He noted the pride, the concern, and had to bow to it. "You have," he admitted. "And I'm grateful." Innate manners took over. "I'm James Parker." He extended his hand.

She observed the gesture as if deliberating over consorting with the enemy. Finally, grudgingly, she accepted it. "I am Luisa Ruggino."

"You're the one who called her *bella*. That's my name for her."

She nodded gravely. "She is a beauty."

"Inside and out," he agreed. "We've been scared to death over her disappearance."

Her expression softened. "She has worried much about her memory. A weaker woman would have been undone."

"Bella has always possessed great inner strength."

A glint of reluctant approval. "She did not sit around pitying herself, though she was badly frightened. She fell apart only once."

"I wish I'd been here for her," he said honestly. Fervently. Sensing that this woman could be obstacle or asset, he made himself vulnerable to her scorn. "I don't know what to do for her. My instinct is to carry her off. Whisk her home."

She studied him with penetrating dark eyes. "She was not one to be ordered about," she guessed.

That provoked a smile. "Never."

"Let me look at your hands," she commanded.

Surprised but not about to risk the delicate truce, he complied.

She studied his palms, first the right, then the left and back again. "A tiny break in your love line." Her gaze lifted. "Some trouble between you."

Inwardly, he quailed, but he brazened it out. "Does any marriage completely escape problems? Bella and I have been together for thirty-six years."

She liked that, he could tell. She released his hands. "My Romeo and I had fifty-four too-short years. I miss him every day." She cast a sly glance. "That does not mean I was not tempted to brain him with a skillet now and again."

James chuckled. "Bella's never taken a pan to me,

but she can definitely fly off the handle. The woman's got a temper, and a hard head to go with it."

"While you are an angel, ever agreeable."

"Nope." He shook his head. "But I'm more inclined to stew, not flare."

"A marriage made in heaven." She grinned.

"Maybe not, but one that's forever." *Please let that be true.*

"For better or worse," the old woman said.

"In sickness and in health," he concurred.

She nodded, seemingly satisfied. "I will not be party to breaking up a marriage, however fond I am of Dr. Sam, but Bella must have time. She is very frightened."

"I won't hurt her." That much was true. He would never again harm her, for one second. If he could have her back, he would be certain not to lose sight of the precious gift she was. "So what do I do? I'm not going back until she can go with me." He surveyed his surroundings. "But I'm not much on idleness. Do you have work I could do for you?"

"I already have Bella for that. She is a very fine cook."

"That she is. And you should see her gardens at home, and the paintings she does. She sews and plays guitar—"

"She has begun making gardens for Dr. Sam. I suspect she does not endure idleness well, either."

He seized on a notion. "Maybe I could help. I have a strong back. Or—" Here he frowned. "Perhaps that's too close?" He despised the uncertainty he felt. "No." He made up his mind. "I'm going to try it. I won't push, but she needs to become accustomed to me again. Or get to know me, maybe I should say." He'd been talking to himself as much as Luisa, but now he faced her. "That's it, isn't it? I have to woo my wife."

"I believe you may." She tapped his arm. "But before you begin demonstrating your muscles, you should have a good breakfast. Come with me. I will feed you."

He grinned. Then hesitated. "Will the good doctor be there?"

"Not this morning. He goes down the mountain to see patients on Tuesdays."

"Not that I'm afraid of him or the competition, you understand." How immature that sounded, a boast. A bluff. "I just don't want to make Bella uncomfortable."

"This will not be a smooth road, James Parker." Her glance was sympathetic. "But I find that the only way to reach your goal is simply to get started."

"I agree." He held out one arm. "Allow me to escort you, madam."

He caught the tiny smile that flirted about her lips.

JANE ROLLED AWAY as the sun speared her eyes. She squeezed them shut and sought the shelter of slumber again.

Then she realized how late it must be, if sunshine had hit her bed. The bulbs. There was a full day's work ahead. She sat up too hastily and had to steady herself.

She inhaled and stretched. Just as suddenly, her arms fell to her sides.

The day before rushed in. She waited for the panic, but instead, what she could remember were the faces. The hope, abruptly extinguished.

She paused and rubbed one temple. Where did they go from here? Oh, she knew what Sam would say: *Take your time. There's no hurry. All that matters is your health.*

But Sam was wrong. Cam, so earnest and sweet, had tugged at her heart. *We need you back, Mom. Home isn't home without you.*

How desperately she wished that evoked even the faintest recall, just one glimpse, shutter-snap quick, that would show her where she'd lived for so long.

When had he lost his first tooth? How had Cele fared in the beginning? Bella must have learned mothering on her—how had she done? She was terrified to hear, lest she'd been a terrible parent, yet the two of them seemed healthy and bright, clearly devoted to James.

To her, as well, however little she felt the same. And wasn't that the worst thing a parent could do, to not feel some visceral connection to her children? Was it because they were adopted? Would things be different if she could spot shared features? Oh, she hoped not. Hadn't they suffered enough, losing the first set of parents?

She had to confront the daughter who viewed her with such disappointment. So much yearning.

And James. He was inexplicably terrifying to her—not a child but a full-grown man, obviously accustomed to exerting his power. Smart and not cruel but altogether too…male. He made her restless beneath her skin. On a simple physical level, he was very attractive to her, but she couldn't accept any of his advances, even if he offered them, for fear of all else she'd become entangled in.

He wasn't simply a potential lover. He was her husband. He held the keys to her home, to her future. If she couldn't remember a career, how could she support herself should he decide he didn't love this new person? But how could she allow herself to be his charity case—or Sam's, for that matter?

Desperate to get out of her thoughts, she walked to the window, twisted open the blinds to check out the morning.

Oh, no. There he was, James. Spading up dirt in the flower bed she'd intended to leave for spring. She nearly said something, but he wouldn't hear her through the glass, anyway.

Then, abruptly, he turned.

Something rippled through her, deeper than conscious thought. Closer than bone.

Eyes locked, minutes passed. Aeons. Some part of her registered the broad shoulders, the long legs encased in jeans. His hair, brushed with silver at the temples, gleamed golden in the morning light. His pupils were a stormy blue.

She retreated from the window and fled to the shower.

SHE VENTURED OUTSIDE at last, arms close to her sides, fingers gripping the seams of her jeans. What had she worn in her other life? She had a moment of nerves, wishing to be more presentable, though she wasn't sure why this man's judgment mattered.

Then she forced herself straight. What she was, who she would be, they would all discover together, it seemed.

"Mornin'." His low drawl was so different from Sam's clipped tones. She enjoyed the music of it.

"Hello." She smiled past her jitters. "I'm, um, I don't usually sleep this late."

"I know," he said. "You always liked to be in your garden early. 'Produce is best picked before the sun hits it, slugabed.' I liked keeping you tucked in beside me as long as I could, but—" He grinned, and she felt a small shiver at the gleam in his eyes. "I was the beneficiary of that drive, so who was I to disagree?"

She strained to remember it. Deflated when she couldn't. "What was my garden like?"

"I should have brought pictures, but I wasn't thinking of anything except how quickly I could get to you." He frowned. "That makes you uncomfortable to hear."

"No, no…" She paused. "Yes, a little. I just regret that I don't—" She halted again.

"Don't feel anything for me?" When she bit her lip, he hastened on. "It's okay. I mean, it's…painful, but it's real. We begin from here and move on."

She cocked her head. "You're a pragmatist."

NO POSTAGE
NECESSARY
IF MAILED
IN THE
UNITED STATES

BUSINESS REPLY MAIL

FIRST-CLASS MAIL   PERMIT NO. 717   BUFFALO, NY

POSTAGE WILL BE PAID BY ADDRESSEE

HARLEQUIN READER SERVICE
3010 WALDEN AVE
PO BOX 1867
BUFFALO NY 14240-9952

Play the Lucky Hearts Game

and get...

2 FREE BOOKS and
2 FREE MYSTERY GIFTS...
YOURS to KEEP!

yes! I have scratched off the silver card. Please send me my *2 FREE BOOKS* and *2 FREE mystery GIFTS* (gifts are worth about $10). I understand that I am under no obligation to purchase any books as explained on the back of this card.

Scratch Here! then look below to see what your cards get you... 2 Free Books & 2 Free Mystery Gifts!

336 HDL ESSM   135 HDL ESVX

FIRST NAME   LAST NAME

ADDRESS

APT.#   CITY

STATE/PROV.   ZIP/POSTAL CODE   (H-SR-07/08)

Twenty-one gets you
**2 FREE BOOKS and
2 FREE MYSTERY GIFTS!**

Twenty gets you
2 FREE BOOKS!

Nineteen gets you
1 FREE BOOK!

TRY AGAIN!

"I thought so, but lately, I'm wondering if I understood anything at all."

"I'm sorry. Is that my fault?"

"No. God, no. You're not to blame for anything." His forehead wrinkled, but he didn't elaborate.

She needed movement. Action. This was getting too uncomfortable. Stifling. She glanced around her, mentally rearranging what she'd envisioned in order to accommodate what he'd done.

She wasn't going to ask him to start over in the garden, too.

"You've got that 'this wasn't what I'd planned' expression." But he was grinning. "I knew better than to just dig in." He chuckled. "Literally. But I was... antsy. We did have that in common, that neither of us could sit still worth a flip." He backed away, held the shovel out to his side. "Say the word, master gardener, and I'll pack all this soil right back down."

He was amazingly good-natured at the prospect. "I had in mind to plant bulbs over there, so that I wouldn't have to dig up so much." She smiled back at him. "This will be better. The plants will probably thank you. That ground is as hard as cement."

"You're telling me." He rubbed his back.

"Have you hurt yourself? Here, let me—"

His laughter brought her up short. "I was only teasing. This is a better workout than the gym. The air is clean and crisp, and I've lost count of how many different types of birdsong I've heard. Anyway, I can handle the dummy end of a shovel fine. Just point me in whatever direction you desire." He swept an imaginary hat from his head and bowed.

She found herself truly smiling for the first time in days. Perhaps they could suit. This was a nice man she'd married.

He smiled at her. For the moment, it was enough.

Then her stomach growled, quite loudly.

"Someone missed breakfast," he said.

"I'll be fine."

He frowned. "You're still healing. You should eat. Anyway, anyone who'd miss one of Luisa's breakfasts is crazy."

"Luisa fed you?"

"She took pity on me when she found me early this morning."

"Where?"

Color flared in his cheeks. "Sleeping in the car."

"Why? I never dreamed—" She realized she had no idea where they'd stay. Lucky Draw had no motel. "Where are the children?"

"Back in Rifle, at the motel."

She frowned. "You left them there?"

"Honey, they're grown. They don't live with us anymore—at least, Cele doesn't. And Cam's only around now and again, less so all the time." A shadow passed over his features.

"You miss them."

"Yeah. So do you. Did," he corrected.

She averted her gaze. "I can't figure—" her voice was barely a whisper "—how a mother could forget

her children." She looked back. "The man she loved."
She drew in a deep breath. "We did love each other?"

His eyes were sadder. "Insanely."

"I'm so sorry."

"Don't." His voice was harsh. "You didn't create
this situation, and if you apologize every time you
can't remember something, we'll never talk about
anything else."

She felt at once affronted and soothed. "You're
right." She nodded. "I'll keep the apologies to a
minimum, as long as you can hear them even when
they're not said."

"You're not the only one who has regrets."

"What for?"

"I wasn't a perfect husband, Bella. I'm only beginning to comprehend how much."

Something in his voice set off a bell of warning.
A tiny ache in her stomach. She didn't know this
man. She must be careful not to make false assump-
tions about him.

But there was a shadow over him that touched her.
The situation had to be incredibly difficult, and no
doubt the children were depending on him for comfort, too.

She would not lean on him yet. Could not afford
to. For all she knew, she would never remember the
life she'd had. It behooved her to proceed with
caution, or she might find herself in some situation
from which she could not extricate herself.

Begin as you mean to continue. Kindness was a

good place. Caution, as well. "Please don't work on this anymore. I'll finish after I've eaten."

"And what would you have me do?"

She hadn't considered his position. "Don't you have to get back to work? What sort of work do you do?"

"I'm not going anywhere without you, Bella." He sounded astonished that she would assume otherwise. "But to answer your question, I own a furniture-manufacturing business in Parker's Ridge, Alabama."

"Aren't you needed there?"

"It doesn't matter. You come first."

"But—" Her heart clutched. So did she have to go already, back to a place she couldn't recall?

He seemed to understand. "I know you're not ready. You don't have to rush, however eager I am to get you home."

"But what about your business?"

"Cele is ready to accept more responsibility. She's returning to be on hand, and we'll do whatever possible via the telephone, since Lucky Draw doesn't appear to have Internet access."

She smiled. "It's a little light on the amenities."

"I've noticed," he said dryly. "And Cam will fly documents back and forth, if necessary, since courier services also appear to be missing in action."

"He mentioned that he was a pilot."

"That would be your doing. Cam has been obsessed with flight since he was old enough to jump off chairs with a towel around his neck."

"Oh, no. Did he hurt himself?"

"Frequently. But never badly enough to discourage him."

"And I thought this was a good idea?"

"No." He smiled. "But you also saw into his heart, when I was busy making plans for him to join me. So you used your wiles on me until I knuckled under."

"Really?"

He laughed. "Okay, so that's an overstatement. You did understand him better, and you gently—and not so gently—insisted that I give him a chance to discover if flying was a fancy or in his blood. So we worked out a compromise. He's in college, however unwillingly, but he's at the airport every second he can manage. He just got his instrument rating a few days ago."

"That's good?"

"That's amazing. I already know that he's not going into partnership with me, though I haven't admitted that to him yet. But, to my surprise, Cele has one hell of a head for business and may just have figured out a way to lead the company into the future."

"You're proud of her."

"Damn proud. Of both of them. We raised two exceptional children."

And she was hurting them. "I need to talk to Cele. Is it too late? Is she gone?"

His expression was pained. "She's taking this hard, though she guards her emotions better than Cam. She's returning home today or tomorrow."

"I...see." She was surprised at how much that hurt.

"But she very much wishes to spend time with you first. She just doesn't want to crowd you."

Her shoulders sagged. Then forcibly, she straightened them. "I'd like time with her, too."

"This is harder on you than any of us," he said.

"Is it?" She studied at him. "I don't think so."

"You're one hell of a woman, Bella. Past and present."

His approval warmed her. "Present is still a mystery, and the past is a black hole. But I'm trying, I promise."

"You're doing great." His voice was so kind. "Now, let's get you some breakfast."

CHAPTER TWELVE

SHE WAS SO NERVOUS she'd already covered up the hole before she realized she'd put no bulb in it. A drop of sweat rolled down her nose and plopped onto the leg of her jeans. She wiped it away impatiently and stabbed her trowel in the dirt to begin again.

"Daddy said you wished to see me." The voice behind her was stiff.

Jane sat back on her heels, prayed for courage. Wished for Cam, his gawky exuberance.

Then she stood. Faced the daughter over whom she towered. Whom she wanted to love because—

Well, because she should.

You're the mother, she chided. *Set the tone.* But she felt blind. Horribly, horribly awkward.

"I did—do," she stumbled. "Good morning, Cele." *Oh, yes, you're doing great. Just grand.* "How are you?" *Any more clichés you'd like to drag out?*

"Fine." Cele stood as stiff as her voice.

"Would you—have you eaten? I could fix you breakfast—"

"I'm not hungry," Cele said in the same instant. "I have to leave soon."

"Oh." Jane's heart hitched. "I, uh—" Then she remembered what James had told her about Cele and the family business. "To return to your work, I guess. Your father's very proud of you. We're proud of you," she amended.

Cele's face grew, if anything, stonier. "There's no need to say that. I know I could be a stranger off the street as far as you're concerned."

"I'm sorry." *Don't apologize. Well, James, that's easy for you to say.* "I don't mean to hurt you. I'm doing all I can to—"

"You didn't call me," Cele blurted. "We talk nearly every day. I was worried sick."

"Oh, Cele—" She longed to go to her, but she was afraid it was the wrong move. Afraid she'd make things worse.

Afraid, afraid, afraid. She was sick to death of living in fear. Always off-balance and scared to take the next step.

Tired of being paralyzed by uncertainty, she moved toward her daughter, who was facing away, arms wrapped around her waist.

Cele had been abandoned in Romania for two years, left to the mercy of baby warehouses and exhausted, ever-changing staffs, James had told her over breakfast.

Did a part of that child always live within the lovely and poised young woman? Compassion had Jane reaching out, laying one hand on Cele's shoulder.

Cele flinched.

Jane withdrew as if she'd been burned. She started to retreat—

But she found herself with an armful of daughter. Being gripped for dear life.

"You called me Muffin," Cele whispered. Her tiny frame shook as she fought to hold back sobs.

Muffin. For a second, an image flickered, then was lost. She grasped for it, a too-quick impression of a little girl with crumbs all around her mouth, a shy grin, a muffin nearly as big as her head clasped in two tiny hands.

When it fled back into the dark maw of her mind, Bella cried out in despair.

Then clutched her daughter to her, instead. "Blueberry."

Cele's head rose swiftly, her eyes filled with hope. "Did you—?"

"You were so small." She thought of the pinched look of the child. "So hungry."

"Daddy bought me a blueberry muffin in the airport. I don't remember it because I was only two, but I've heard the story a million times." Longing spilled over her lashes in a silvery stream. "Do you remember that, Mama?"

She fought her own tears. Wanted to give assurances that she should not. "It was so fast, just a little flash, but…"

"But you remembered me." Cele's voice was wonder. Excitement. Cele drew away, then hugged her tightly again. "Mama, you remembered me. It's coming back."

"Not—" Enough. Not nearly enough. She warmed in her daughter's embrace and struggled to find another light in the black hole that was her mind, something of Cam, of…him. James. But even that too-swift flare of Cele was gone, and she sought for it so desperately that she felt in danger of tumbling back into the dreaded darkness.

She recoiled from the edge of the cliff.

Cele withdrew. "Are you okay?" Her daughter's eyes shone so brightly, so wistfully that she couldn't bear to disappoint her.

"I'm fine," she said, running one hand over Cele's fair hair. "Muffin."

Cele's smile was the sun. "Let's go find Daddy and Cam and tell them."

Expectations can do more harm than good. Bella shivered under the cloud of Sam's warning.

But she smiled at the happy girl tugging on her hand. "Let's do."

SHE STOOD APART from the three of them, the father, so comfortable in his role, so easy with his affection where she was still frozen. James had one arm slung around his son's neck and his daughter tucked into the other side. The unity was beautiful to watch.

Painful, too.

Even if she could reclaim every second they'd shared in full, glorious color, would the distance that was now a gaping wound heal into only a tiny scar? Or, better, vanish altogether?

What happens when a trust is abridged? She couldn't recall her own mother, but common sense told her that the bond was unique, that a mother should be someone you can count on, no matter what. Your most vocal cheerleader, your unwavering comfort. The go-to person for sharing both trouble and joy.

Yet she'd vanished from their lives for days upon days that became weeks. Failed, as Cele's heartrending question illuminated, to even bother with a phone call.

Best Jane could determine, she'd been gone nearly a week when The Incident had happened, the one nobody was ready to discuss. Why had she not phoned them during that time?

Then, of course, she couldn't. She'd been injured, badly enough to lose consciousness. To have who she was ripped out at the most basic level.

But she wouldn't think on that now. The point was, she had children. A husband. For whatever reason she'd been traveling, she hadn't kept in touch with any of them, not even once a day.

What did that, so cold and uncaring, say about who she was? How could they love her if she'd been that callous?

"Mom?" Cam paused before her. "You okay?" He worried about her all the time now, this boy who should be focusing on girls and having fun.

"Fine." She smiled. Cradled his cheek. Already, he was dear to her, however unfamiliar. "Do you have a girlfriend?"

"Mom!" Behind him, James chuckled and Cele grinned.

"What? Isn't a mother supposed to ask these things?"

But the joke fell flat. The wound was still too raw, all of them exceedingly aware that this question was hardly rhetorical.

She glanced away. "I was just...I'm eager to get to know you, that's all."

"I'm sorry," he said hastily.

"No, don't be." She rebounded, pasted on a smile. "We'll figure this out. I promise I'll get better." Though her doubts were bigger than these mountains.

"Sure you will. You remembered Cele's muffin, right? And me as a baby. It's a start."

But she was only too aware of the person she did not recall, unless a mental picture of a hand counted.

James's gaze was solemn as it met hers.

Then he winked and bolstered her with a reassuring smile, as if to say *we'll get there*.

"That's right." She grabbed Cam fiercely. "Do your homework," she said gruffly to battle back tears.

His laughter, all of theirs, was a little ragged.

She let Cam cling, but opened one arm to Cele, who moved into the embrace and held on tight.

For a moment, the warmth of them, of their longing, their sorrow, their love, was light in her darkness. A flame to ward off the predators that were her loneliness, her isolation. Her despair.

She wept for what they had lost, all of them, even as she drank in the sweet surrender children grant to those who care for them.

Within her arose a powerful resolve to fight for this, for them, these hearts that, despite everything, wanted to trust her. Needed her back.

Finally, she made herself let them go when she yearned to cling. To fall to the ground from weariness.

She sniffed and managed a smile, noting that both of them were crying, as well. She grasped a hand from each and squeezed. "Look up and down."

They were thunderstruck, as was James.

"You always said that," Cele told her. "Every time we'd go anywhere. You said it came from your grandfather, a reference to watching before you crossed train tracks."

The hope in their eyes was blinding.

"It's gonna work, Mom," Cam said.

"Yes." For the first time, she began to believe it herself.

She smiled and kissed each of their cheeks, letting her hands trail away, a stroke down the arm, a brush of the hand. "Now, get on the road while there's still daylight, and—" *You didn't call me.* Did she dare ask?

Absolutely. "Phone me when you get there, will you?"

Sun-bright smiles, and one more hug for their father, then reluctant steps to the car.

She waved until they could no longer possibly spot her, but she had this sense that if she kept her hand high despite screaming muscles, the benediction would hold. The plea to whoever ruled these mountains that her children would be safe, as she herself had not been.

"Well, it's just us now." She hadn't realized James had walked up behind her until he spoke.

She couldn't help taking one step to the side.

Shattering the warmth of the moment.

She didn't know why he made her so nervous. He hadn't been anything but kind to her.

He was so big, so handsome, so…somehow threatening, and she couldn't figure it out.

"Yes," she acknowledged, but couldn't think what else to say.

The silence was anything but comfortable.

He sighed. "Listen, I'd better, uh, make some calls."

She had the sense that what he really wanted was to get away from her, and she didn't protest. She was too raw, too buffeted by emotions.

"I, um…" She glanced around, then seized on the first thing that popped into her mind. "I'll be helping Luisa can some beans." Though she wasn't at all certain Luisa hadn't already finished.

Even if she could remember her past, she couldn't imagine that she'd had any moments more awkward than this. "Um, see you later?"

One small shake of the head and an attempt at a smile. "Sure."

She'd let him down again, that couldn't be more evident in his walk. She rubbed her forehead, where a headache was brewing. She would be true to her word and check if Luisa needed anything.

But she could barely put one foot in front of the other and thought longingly of the cool darkness of her bedroom and the oblivion, however temporary, it offered.

HE SHOULD HAVE GONE with the kids. What was he thinking? Just when she seemed to leap a barrier and he was filled with the same hope he noted in his children's eyes, when he'd thought they could make some real progress together—

The kids left, and she turned to stone.

Not only did she not love him, he wasn't at all certain she even liked him. He'd thought differently at breakfast, but…

Did she sense, somehow? Did a part of her know?

He glanced back, where she was walking away, her footsteps dragging. Slow, as if weighed down by grief.

His heart sank. They were having exactly the negative effect Lincoln had warned about. Maybe he should go. Leave her alone.

To do so went against his every instinct. It was his job in life to protect her, to slay her dragons. To shield her from all harm.

But what if he was the chief danger?

James bowed his head. For most of their life together, he and Bella had been completely honest with each other. She was his best friend as much as his lover. There had been no reason to hold back on anything more important than a birthday surprise.

When had all that changed? How had the shift escaped his notice?

She was nearly to the guest quarters, about to disappear from his sight. He longed to race to her, say anything, do whatever was required to be allowed to go inside with her. To pour out his heart, tell her everything. Spend hours, days, weeks catching her up, making her understand that what they had was rare and good and so beautiful that it must continue, had to be saved.

James laughed at himself without mirth. So, exactly how would he begin this recitation? *Bella, you love me even if you don't remember it, and I cherish you more than my life. There's just this one thing that happened, and for the life of me, I can't say how I got to that point, but you have to believe me.*

How could she? Why *should* she?

He sagged against the post of the back porch of his enemy's house and watched his heart vanish from sight.

Sam Lincoln wasn't his enemy, however; James himself owned that distinction.

Not many things had ever made him want to cry, but the thought of losing Bella went deeper than tears, a dread that sank into his bones. Poisoned him to the marrow.

He shoved away. Damned if he'd go down without

a fight. James Parker did not give up on anything he really desired, and there was nothing on earth he craved more than Bella.

He stared at the dirt they'd both touched this morning. Thought about the energy he would have to burn off to get calm.

He'd plant the rest of those bulbs for her, but he would do something more, something better. Something that would lift her heart.

He heard Luisa in the kitchen behind him, and a crafty smile spread.

He went inside to enlist an ally.

WHEN BELLA OPENED the door, her curls were sleep tumbled, so familiar and beloved that it was all James could do not to grab her there and then. Bury his face in those curls, wrap his body around hers, sweet-talk her back into bed.

Down, boy. "I woke you. I'm sorry."

She glanced at the basket in his hand, then back at him. "No sorrys, remember?" Her voice was husky, and it brought back too many memories of waking her with kisses, slipping inside her before she was fully conscious. Or having her do the same, sliding down onto him with a wicked grin.

He closed his eyes to shield his thoughts from her. She was a long way from ready.

"James?"

"Yeah?"

"You all right?"

No. He was busy beating back his body's reaction to her. "Sure." Lifted the basket. "Now that I've messed up your nap, not that I'm using that S word, of course—" he was relieved to see her smile back "—how about a picnic?"

"Picnic," she echoed, as if he'd spoken a foreign language.

"Yeah, you know, sandwiches, potato chips—" he held up his other hand "—blanket?" *Grapes I eat from your fingers after I've stripped you naked and made you scream.*

He cleared his throat. "Actually, it's a little more than just sandwiches. Luisa didn't approve of all my choices. But I made what you like—peanut butter and sweet pickles."

"You…made." Then her nose wrinkled. "Peanut butter and…sweet pickles?"

"Oh." The wind went out of his sails. "I didn't think about your tastes changing." He let his arm drop. "I could fix something else."

But her eyes had gone soft. "No, please." And she touched him. Voluntarily. "Don't alter anything." Though she looked doubtful.

"I chose ham for me. I'll share if you don't like yours."

"James…" Her lip trembled just a little.

"Hey, now. You don't have to go. I just thought…" He shrugged. "Luisa said you've been working a lot, and you hadn't spent any time just fooling around, so—" He felt miserably inept.

"You cooked for me."

He had to resist the urge to shuffle his feet and say *aw, shucks*. "Cooking might be an overstatement. You're the whiz in the kitchen."

She touched his forearm again, so brief and light he might have imagined it, had he not been looking.

He felt it like a brand.

"I'd…like to go. If you don't mind allowing me a minute to get ready."

Relief rushed through him until he was light-headed. "You're worth the wait."

Color flared on her cheeks. "I'll be quick."

"I'll be here."

She hesitated, and he realized that he was standing inside the doorway.

He'd rather not, but he stepped back. He'd have to earn the right to watch her perform those female rituals he'd once taken for granted, even been impatient over now and again.

Another bittersweet image assaulted him, Bella in lingerie, chatting about the day's events while brushing her teeth, as if they'd experienced those moments so often and would in the future that there was no reason to make note of them.

What he wouldn't give for one of them, just one, however mundane.

The footing was so treacherous here. He had to fight for every inch of ground, and all could be lost in the blink of an eye, it seemed.

But she'd said yes. He'd advanced his flag,

however tiny the increment. Viewed from here, his goal might as well be Mount Everest.

Progress it was, however, and he'd be thankful for it.

CHAPTER THIRTEEN

"HERE—" He extended a hand. "This descent could be a little dicey."

She hesitated, and he glanced back at her, patience vying with frustration over her continued skittishness. Her hesitation was not, however, for the reason he probably imagined. She did not fear him. He'd been kind and gentle, had gone out of his way to be considerate.

She feared herself. The strength of her attraction to him, however ridiculous it was to be nervous around your husband of thirty-six years.

He started to withdraw his hand.

She grabbed it. Held on tight. Met his gaze… and lingered.

James drew her down the slope with exquisite care. Surveyed to be certain no peril waited, before he focused on her.

His gaze dipped to her mouth and back. And again. He said not a word, but the heat in his eyes scorched her.

Something passed between them, so fierce, so

vividly alive she wondered why the trees didn't burst into flame. She chewed on her lower lip, and his disappointment flickered.

He turned and once more led the way, toting the picnic basket and blanket as if they were nothing.

She pressed one palm to her stomach and reminded herself to breathe. She wanted that kiss too much from a man she barely knew, however intimate he was with the details of her past.

This roller coaster was wearing her out, the up and down of hope and fear, the nagging uncertainty about who she was, where she belonged.

She took a step into the future to wrest control back. To find what they could be together. "Have we ever been on a picnic before?" she asked his broad back, admiring the look of him. He kept himself fit, commendably so. He was terribly appealing to her. Did her body remember better than her mind?

"Lots of times," he said. "I met you in a tree."

"What?" She stumbled on a rock, began sliding.

He caught her. Held her close. Once more, the pull strengthened, the invisible cord, crackling with energy, tightened.

She resisted the urge to lay her palms on his chest. To dig her fingers into the muscle. To lay her head on his shoulder and...take shelter.

The longing she saw in his expression undid her. Gingerly, she touched his cheek with her fingertips. "I don't know you, but..."

"Some part of you does." His voice was gravel. "Let me kiss you, Bella. I'm dying."

Caution held her fast. But the plea she saw… heard… He was her husband. She leaned closer, but only the merest inch.

"Is that a yes?" Husky still, his voice nonetheless ceded control. "I won't force you, Bella. Not ever."

A good man. Her *husband*.

She made the first move. "Yes." She laid her lips on his. Braced for the impact of his obvious eagerness.

Instead, he rubbed his mouth over hers softly…so very softly. Tickled her. Made her burn.

She found herself taking the kiss further as he waited so patiently, as if he had all the time in the world. As if this kiss were everything, and he would not rush his fences.

"Mmm," she hummed deep in her throat.

His arm wrapped around her, but he didn't drop the picnic basket and blanket. Didn't throw her to the ground.

However much the tension in his frame told her he wished to do exactly that.

The one arm around her waist tightened, though. Brought her into his body, the length of it, the easy power. She felt his response to her, and that emboldened her to slick her tongue over the seam of his lips, swirl the tip just inside them.

James groaned, and his arm was a steel band.

But still he didn't rush her, didn't press.

Her own body was way ahead of her, shouting for

her mind to keep up. She fell into the glory of this, the luxury of touch, of surcease for her skin's hunger for contact. For grounding.

She tilted her head and deepened the kiss, tempted to beg him to take over, while relishing the sheer pleasure of this feeling that, for the first time since she'd awakened, the choice was hers, the power hers to wield.

"James," she murmured. "Kiss me back."

He dropped the basket and the blanket then. And did as she asked.

She was lost then, adrift on a swell of heat and hope and rapture, of endless possibilities with such life roaring through her veins, burning her up, sending her spiraling into space, then falling, falling until she couldn't get her footing, couldn't tell where she was in the dizzy, swirling void.

"No!" she gasped. Pushed away. "I can't go back. Can't—" She retreated, searching for her bearings, reeling from the sense that she was descending once more into the darkness.

He was visibly horrified. "What are you saying? You won't go home? Are you telling me—"

"No—I didn't mean—" She shut her eyes. Struggled for sanity. "I'm sorry." Oh, God. What had she done?

"Sorry we kissed?" His face was a mask of confusion. Of shame. "I wasn't—I wouldn't hurt you, Bella." Pain vied with humiliation, and she was sick at heart for what she'd done with a moment so precious.

"It's me, James, not you. I—panicked."

"You're afraid." His voice was hollow. "Of…*me?*"

"No." She shook her head frantically. "Of—I don't know. For a second, I was so lost, and I couldn't get my balance. It was too much like that dizziness, that terrible—" She cast her eyes down, fighting tears. "It's stupid. I screwed everything up, and I'm so sorry."

"Shh…" His tone was tender as his fingers touched her chin, tilted it up. A wistful smile curved his lips. "It's sort of flattering, you realize. I've read the phrase *he kissed her senseless,* but I never imagined I'd be able to make that claim."

"I'm such a mess," she said, and wanted to wail.

"You're not." He brushed at her damp cheeks. "Anyway, you're my mess."

She blinked. *I love that mess.*

"My hair." She could barely breathe. "It was you who said it was my glory." Her heart raced. "I said it was a mess, and you argued that it was—"

His smile was huge, his eyes shining. He squeezed them shut for a second, then swooped her up and twirled her around, before stopping to crush her into his embrace. "I was afraid you'd never remember me." His voice cracked, and she fought back tears. He buried his face in her neck, and she could feel him tremble. She tightened her arms around him awkwardly, desperately guilty about causing him so much pain. Humbled by the depth of it.

Frightened of hurting him more. "James…I still don't—"

His arms gripped her. "I know," he murmured into

her throat. "I understand." His voice had gone dull. "There's a long way yet."

His head lifted, and he looked at her, all pretenses gone. "I'm doing my best to be patient. I won't let you down." It was a promise, earnest and heartfelt. "But you can't imagine what it means." His voice dropped. "I thought I'd lost you." Haunted eyes gazed at her. "I've made mistakes, Bella, but I swear I've loved you with everything in me. I'll do whatever is required to get you back."

How could she remain unmoved in the face of this? Why couldn't she remember, damn it? "I'm doing my best."

"I wasn't saying—" He set her down but kept her close. "Bella, I know you are. I just— I feel so much for you, and I'm used to having my feelings returned." His gaze bored into hers. "But I'll wait, I swear it. However long you need, I'll be here. You're not alone in this, sweetheart." He clasped her hands between his strong ones. Brought them to his lips as though sealing a pledge. "For better or for worse, in sickness and in health," he said. "Whether you recall the marriage vows or not, I do."

"I'm so sorry," she whispered. "I've hurt you. I don't want to."

"Shh." He pressed one finger to her lips. "I can handle it." He studied her. "You're tired. I'll take you back." To his credit, he kept all but a trace of the disappointment out of his tone. He bent and picked up the basket and the blanket.

"No." She grasped his forearm, this time accepting that the feel of him was reassuring, not frightening.

"You're exhausted."

"I can nap. That's what people do after a picnic, right?"

"Sometimes. But you're still on the mend."

"I'm not an invalid." She crossed her arms over her chest. "Now, do I get my picnic or not?"

Still he hesitated. "Bella, it's not a good idea to strain your limits."

Something in her balked at the babying. "You can't stop me from hiking."

His eyes widened. "Wanna bet?" Then his smile spread. "I guess some things are hardwired."

"What do you mean?"

"You never did a damn thing I asked you unless you wanted to." He chuckled. "I never imagined I'd feel grateful for your stubborn streak."

"I'm not stubborn." She sniffed.

His laughter rang out once more. "And your hair's not curly, either." He tugged at one lock, and his expression became serious. "You are still the most beautiful woman I've ever seen."

She ducked her head, oddly shy now. She searched for a diversion.

Then she recalled what he'd said earlier. "So what's this about meeting me in a tree?"

He grasped her hand and headed toward their picnic, not back to Sam's, and she smiled. "Well, now, that's a long story."

"We've got time."

He glanced over his shoulder. "Yeah. We do." He squeezed her fingers and led her on.

JAMES WATCHED her take the first bite gingerly, as though it might be laced with arsenic. A glimpse of even, white teeth, then her lips closing over the bread.

Man. He was getting hard just seeing her eat a sandwich. He was so bad off.

She chewed for a second. Then she brightened like the sun. "It's good," she marveled. "Really good."

Happiness flooded him. A new connection made, another brick pulled from the wall that separated them. He laughed from relief and hope, flopped over on his back on the blanket. Above him was blue sky framed by tall firs, and suddenly, all seemed right with the world, however far they had yet to travel.

Maybe that was the trick, to stop and enjoy each precious moment. He'd always forged ahead, clearing a trail to provide safe passage for his family and his company. He'd spent little time in the present, too focused on the future.

"You seem happy," she said.

"I am."

"Because I like your sandwich?"

He rolled back to his side, propped on one elbow. "Because I love you so much I can't breathe sometimes." Before she could shy away as he could tell she was about to, he backed off. "Certainly not because I admire your taste in sandwiches. That one is beyond weird."

"Try it." She held it out to him, the spot where her lips had been.

He yearned to place his own there, seal a connection.

But not bad enough to eat that godforsaken concoction. "Trust me, I have. Several times." He gave a theatrical shudder. "You've brought so much color into my life, Bella, and I'm more grateful than I can say." He pointed. "But not that grateful."

She laughed from deep in her belly, and his mouth curved into a wide smile.

"Do the kids like it?"

"Cele used to eat it with grim determination because she wanted to be like her mommy. Cam tried one bite and spit it out. No one on earth likes that hideous creation but you."

"Did I already eat it when we met?"

"Yes, but if I'd known… I mean, it was obvious you were unique, but—" He shook his head. "That combination is another matter altogether."

"What do you mean, unique?"

"How long do you have?" When her forehead wrinkled, he smiled to reassure her. "You caught my attention the first second I saw you, and I never looked back. I had to have you. Even though I had a girlfriend at the time."

"Ouch."

"Yeah, well, she and I would never have made it

past high school." But Beth had been exactly what he'd believed he wanted.

Until Bella.

"How old were we?" Then her eyes popped. "I just realized I don't know my age. Sam and I guessed somewhere in my fifties."

"Fifty-seven. Your birthday is August second."

"How old are you?"

"Fifty-eight."

"And your birthday?"

"January sixteenth."

"A Capricorn, and I'm a Leo." She frowned. "How can I recall that about astrology and not—?"

He longed to understand that himself, but he cared more about erasing the sadness on her face. "Leo and Capricorn...a combustible mix." He waggled his eyebrows.

A little of her sorrow melted away.

"You said you were seventeen when we met. Where was that?"

"My high school in Parker's Ridge. You were the new girl."

"Do I have family? Besides you and the kids, I mean?"

He grimaced. "No. I'm sorry. You had come to live with a cousin of your dad's, but she passed away four years ago."

"My parents?"

"I don't think you ever knew your father. Your mother—"

"What is it?"

"She's gone now, but she was unstable, from what you told me. She drifted in and out of your life."

"Where did I spend the time in between?"

"You were bounced around a lot." He hesitated, not eager to disturb the temporary peace.

"Why?"

"Bella, it's not important. It was a long time ago."

"James, please don't hide my past from me. What aren't you saying?"

"Nothing bad, I swear." He hastened to reassure her. "You were simply a little…rebellious."

"How rebellious?"

He exhaled. "You'd been thrown out of three schools. But it's perfectly understandable, considering the upheaval you'd experienced. You just needed a steady source of love."

She studied him. "You became that, didn't you?"

He shrugged. "We grew up together."

"No. One thing I've learned from observing you the past few days is that you're steady, James. A rock for others."

He squirmed inwardly. "Not always."

"I think you are. You're a protector. I notice the way you watch over the kids, how they look to you and trust you. And I've experienced your kindness firsthand."

"I've made mistakes, don't kid yourself. Big ones." He waited for her to ask what he meant.

But she didn't. "So tell me about the tree."

"Tree?" Still caught in the grip of fear, he needed a minute to catch up. "Oh. That tree." He couldn't help but grin. "You had the best damn legs I ever saw. Still do."

She blushed. "Why was I in a tree?"

"Beats me. I gave up long ago on figuring out why you do anything." And wasn't that part of the problem? That he'd somehow quit truly seeing her?

Well, he saw her now, and he wanted her more than ever. Yearned to clear things between them, to admit what he'd done and ask for her forgiveness. Explain somehow, though he didn't really understand, himself. The man who could have faltered, even for a second, in his devotion to Bella was a stranger to him.

Their rapport was so new. So fragile. She'd had a lot thrown at her already. As soon as he was a little more certain of their bond, when she'd had time to feel the depth of his love for her and could understand—

"Tell me what happened next."

He yanked his thoughts away from where their paths had diverged and instead began describing to her the scene of their first meeting. How the cocky quarterback had walked away from the rebel but hadn't been able to get her out of his mind.

She followed the recitation with mixed expressions, surprise and chagrin, with something that resembled admiration.

But he noticed her tiring, and he realized that to begin to summarize their life together would require days, weeks even.

"Enough," he said. "We've got time to cover all that ground. Anyway, I have to get back in case Cele has called."

"Oh." She scrambled up, began gathering the remnants. "Your business. I forget that it's there. It doesn't seem quite real to me yet."

His mouth quirked. "Seems all too real to me."

Her hands stilled. "Is it burdensome, what you do?"

He shrugged. "I have people who are depending on me for their livelihood."

"You take your responsibilities very seriously, don't you?"

"It's what a man does."

"Not all men. I may have no memory of our past, but I think you shoulder burdens others wouldn't." She caught his gaze. "Like me. From what I heard of your conversation with Cele before they left, there are business concerns you should be dealing with instead of staying here."

He leaned closer. "Nothing is more important than you. Nothing." Somehow he'd lost sight of that, until he faced losing her.

"But what about the business?"

"Cele and I will handle it just fine. I'm not leaving here, Bella, until I can have you with me."

She went quiet, then, "Should we go now?"

But he could hear her unease. "Not before you're ready. I'll deal with the company long distance."

"Do you like your work, James?"

Did he? "That's not important."

"Why do you do it, then?"

Good question. "It's my legacy. The company was founded by my great-grandfather."

"So you grew up in the business?"

"Oh, yeah. From the time I was little, I knew where my future would be. My dad started me at the bottom, when I was ten, sweeping up the shop floor after the day ended."

"Then what?"

"I learned, step by step, about working with wood, though much of it was in my blood. I'd been hanging around with my dad in his home workshop since I was very small. I'd made a table of my own design by the time I was nine." He grinned. "I still have it. The artistry's not much, but it's still holding. Cele and Cam used it in their playhouse."

"You like the woodworking. The creativity."

"Yeah. I do." He missed that. "Some of the company's most popular pieces are my designs."

She cocked her head. "Do you still work in wood?"

"Me?" He shook his head. "No. No time."

"Maybe you should. Just for pleasure. I have a sense that you don't grant yourself much of that."

He frowned at her insight. When he tried to recall what he did besides work and worry, he couldn't. He hadn't recognized how much the company had become his life.

"Do you have a workshop at home?"

He nodded. "Gathering dust."

"Did you ever make anything for me?"

"The rocking chair you used for Cele and Cam. Your jewelry box. Other things." Like much of the cabinetry in their house and several key pieces of furniture.

"I wish I could see them," she said.

You can. Come with me now. Let's go home. All of these were on the tip of his tongue, but he was not going to push her, and he realized something more.

This was the first vacation he'd had in a very long time. An unconventional one, to be sure, courting a wife who didn't remember him. And certainly not the best time to be away.

But he'd been absolutely sincere. Nothing mattered more than Bella. He'd do his part in the business from here, whatever was required, but he was not budging.

And in the meantime, he had a beautiful woman with him in an isolated spot, what most men would consider a dream getaway.

That the woman and he were not sharing quarters, that she had a guard dog in Sam Lincoln, that there was still a reckoning ahead…well, so the situation wasn't perfect.

He was here. Bella was with him.

It was a good beginning.

"I'd like to show them to you." He picked up the basket and held out his hand to her. "Ready?"

When she accepted it without hesitation, everything suddenly seemed possible.

CHAPTER FOURTEEN

"COME ON IN, JAMES," she called out at the knock on her door. He'd left to phone Cele and said he had an errand to run afterward. He must have completed both in record time.

She ducked into the bathroom for a quick check of her hair before greeting him. "It's nice that you like my curls as they are, because—"

Sam, not James, stood just inside the room.

She faltered. "Oh. Hi, Sam. I thought you were—"

"Yeah, I could tell." He scrutinized her. "How are you?"

"I'm fine."

He didn't look convinced. "Luisa said you were gone all afternoon, that you went on a picnic. Did you go far? You're still recovering your strength. You shouldn't overdo."

She approached him, held out both hands and took his in them. "Stop worrying over me, Sam. James took excellent care of me. Watched me like a hawk. Like I was fine china." *As if I was precious.*

Abruptly, she recalled what had happened and

squeezed his hands, ready to dance a jig. "Sam, I remembered him. How he—" She felt her face warm at the memory of James's eyes so full of her, so dark with longing. She glanced away from Sam, keeping the intimacy to herself. "And Cele— I called her Muffin because when we brought her home, James bought her one in the airport, and she had crumbs all—" She smiled at him. "It's going to return, isn't it? Everything's going to be just fine."

"How much have you remembered?"

"Something about each of them. And James told me how we met and about his business and the rocking chair he made for the nursery—"

"Slow down. Your pulse is racing. You're getting overexcited."

She hadn't noticed that he'd been checking her wrist. She yanked her hands back. "I'm not a child, Sam. And I don't need a keeper." At the hurt on his face, she softened. "I'm sorry. You've been more than wonderful to me. I owe you my life. It's not that I don't appreciate everything, but I just…" She threw up her hands. "I have to know where I belong."

"I'm not out to be a wet blanket." A quick grin. "Okay, I am, but only because I care about you." Something flared in his eyes. "More than a doctor should, I'm afraid."

"Oh, Sam." She bit her lip. "You're such a good man, and if I wasn't—"

"Married?" A shake of his head. "Trust me, I'm only too aware of that little impediment. Figures that when I finally meet the woman who could tempt me out of my bachelorhood, some other guy would already have a claim on her."

Chagrin and delight mingled. "Sam, I'm fifty-seven. You're what—forty-five?"

"Forty-four, but who's counting?"

"I'm much too old for you."

"Your age doesn't mean a thing to me." His expression was serious. "I respect you too much to sabotage that bond, once it's real for you again. But that doesn't mean I'm going to just stand back and let him take advantage of you." He held up a hand at her protest. "Hear me out. He may be exactly what you want, and you may slide seamlessly back into the life you had, but there is absolutely no guarantee of that. I will not allow him to pressure you into leaving before you're ready, and that you are not. Not yet. You could very well remember not one other bit of your past, or you could regain it all tomorrow, but however that plays out, you won't be the same person you were before the accident."

She shook her head to deny that possibility.

"You may not like hearing that, but it's true. Something big has happened to you, and the impact of it will not go away simply because you wish it. You may find out that your old life doesn't fit, and that James is not the man for you."

She couldn't breathe. She'd begun to pin her hopes on regaining her memory and slipping back into the world of Cam and Cele and James, the way you don a much-loved, comfortable shoe. "He's a decent man, Sam, a kind one. He loves me. My children love me. They need me."

"But what do you need?" He saw too deeply. "You don't know that yet, and you ignore it at your peril. There is still danger for you, and this headlong rush into a life in which you might not have been so happy is foolhardy, however badly you wish to believe it."

"No. Sam, you're wrong." She backed away.

"Am I?" He followed. "Why were you this far from your family? Why did they have no idea where you were?"

Her head pounded. "But they—" Little dots danced before her eyes. "They love me. I'm sure of it." She couldn't seem to get a breath.

"Sit down. God, I'm sorry." He drew her gently toward the bed, knelt beside her. "Look at me, warning you of the pressure, then placing even more on you myself. Put your head between your knees." He felt her pulse again. "Deep breaths." Pulled his stethoscope from his pocket. "Talk to me. Even if I am a total jerk."

She found a smile. Lifted her head. "I'm okay."

He busied himself listening to her heart, her lungs. "I'll be the judge of that. I ought to be good for something. I'm obviously a bust as a shrink."

He sounded so upset with himself that she placed one hand on his forearm. "You're only trying to be careful of me."

"Doing a great job, too, aren't I?" He huffed out

a long breath. "Okay, I get points for meaning well, but I lose even more for scaring a patient into hyperventilating. Score for Dr. Sam—minus two hundred on a scale of one to twenty-five."

"Don't be so hard on yourself. I do appreciate your caution." She averted her gaze. "And you're right. I long to feel what he does when he looks at me." She glanced up. "He really loves me, Sam. It's not my imagination. And the kids…they're wonderful. Cele was tough at first, but she was frightened. She needs me a great deal, I think. And Cam—what a sweetheart. They're both bright and thoughtful, and they love James so much and depend on him." She grimaced. "I believe too many people depend on him. He's so conscientious, and he has a lot of responsibilities he's juggling. I suspect he doesn't allow himself to think about his own desires because he's so busy caring for others. I don't want to be a burden on him."

"Doesn't sound as if he considers you that. He damn sure doesn't appear to be here against his will."

"He says he's not leaving until I'm ready." At Sam's mutter of protest, she explained, "He's not pushing, Sam, I swear it. He's bent over backward to be cautious with me, even when…" The memory of James's ardor, of how breathless he could make her feel, had her blushing again.

"I'll have a talk with him. I'm not sure you're ready to resume physical relations."

"Sam!" This was so awkward.

"I'm a doctor. I am aware that people have sex."

"I won't discuss this with you, except to say that yes, I'm very attracted to him, but he has not taken advantage of that, even though it's obvious that ours was…" Where was the girl he'd called a rebel now? She felt like a Victorian prude, talking about her sex life with another man. "A strong physical bond as well as an emotional one."

He squatted in front of her. "But you don't feel those bonds yet, do you? You believe they exist only because he tells you about them. That's exactly why you have to exercise caution. You have to learn this man for yourself. Understand him for who he is, not who he once was to you." His forehead wrinkled. "I'm saying this as your doctor, not as a rival for your affections. There is a distinct possibility that you will never uncover that marker to go back to where you were. You have to learn whether the man who says he's your husband is a man you would fall in love with today. Otherwise, you're cheating both of you."

"But, Sam, the children—"

"They're not children, Jane."

Bella, she began to protest, but James had told her that was only his name for her. She would keep that private to them. Make a new beginning with it. "Isabella, Sam. I have a name now."

"Isabella." He seemed pained. "They're young adults who are making their own lives. Yes, they love you and need you to an extent, but they're not going to be a part of your daily existence in the same way little ones are. The life you have to fit into is with James, and it's not that uncommon for couples to grow apart once the kids are gone."

"But—"

"I'm not saying that's true of the two of you, but you can't argue the case either way. The point is moot. Your past may or may not come back to you, so you must choose your life for what it is now. Take a good hard look at this man. Figure out who he really is and whether that appeals to you, because even if you regain every last memory, you are not going to be exactly the same person you were before the blow to your head. The Bella of today has to determine if the James of today is the right man for her. And he'll have to do likewise." He shoved to his feet. "And now, I've said too much and burst the lovely bubble you were floating in. I'd tell you I'm sorry, and I am, a little, but mostly, I have to make certain that this lovely creature who is under my protection receives it for as long as she requires it."

"Thank you," she said. But she wasn't sure how much she meant it.

"I've made you unhappy, and I regret that. But I'd regret it more if you left too soon and found yourself more unhappy back there."

Her eyes swam. "How will I know if I don't try?"

"I'd sell my soul for a crystal ball right now." He walked to the door. "I apologize for making you sad and wiping away that happy smile you were wearing when you thought I was James." He turned away, then back. "But I won't apologize for protecting you."

She didn't know what to say to that, but it didn't matter.

He was gone before she got the chance.

And she was left to ponder her next step.

JAMES HAD TO HIKE off his restlessness before he saw Bella again. He'd untangled a couple of knotty issues for Cele and put together a request list for Cam's flight back tomorrow morning. He didn't want Cam to be distracted from his schoolwork by traveling here too often, but the new chinks in the wall between him and Bella had made him impatient, however much he struggled to be otherwise.

So he was stacking the deck in his favor. If he couldn't take Bella home, he would bring home to her, as much as possible. The kids would gather up her paints and guitar, the CDs she played most and her favorite clothes, along with some of that Belgian chocolate she adored. Not so much she'd be overwhelmed.

But triggers, each one of them—at least, that was the hope. Guideposts to lead her back to him.

Night was near. Sam Lincoln, her Cerberus, would be watching the gates.

James could not bring himself to put fifty miles between him and Bella again, so…the car it was. He would buy blankets and return as quickly as—

He halted. A little cabin ahead, seemingly deserted. He hiked over, peered in the grimy windows.

It wasn't much, only one room, long uninhabited, he would guess. Who did it belong to, stuck out here away from everyone?

A slow smile spread over his face. Away. From everyone. A place to be with Bella, to spend time alone.

The door was padlocked, but he did as thorough a survey as possible from outside, making mental notes of what he would need.

Please let this one thing go right. Let me find the owner and arrange to lease it.

Luisa. She liked him, and she believed in the sanctity of marriage. She would help. He wasn't too proud to beg.

James drove back to Lucky Draw with a lighter step.

HE'D SLEPT in his car last night, he'd said. Where was he now?

Bella was aware of a surprising sense of disappointment that she hadn't encountered James again after the picnic. He hadn't exactly promised to come back once he'd spoken with Cele, but the way he'd behaved, she'd assumed...

Where was he?

Some evenings she'd enjoyed watching television with Sam, losing herself to the dramas of other lives or the foolishness of sitcoms.

Tonight she'd begged off after dinner, citing weariness. She'd thought she wanted to be alone to sort out all that had happened in the past two days.

Instead, she realized that she'd been expecting

James to drop by. Was eager to hear more about the life they'd shared.

Wouldn't mind another kiss.

But she'd recoiled from the first one—hardly the response he would have hoped for. Again and again he'd made overtures that she'd dodged.

How long would he persist?

I'm not leaving here until I can take you with me. You may find out that your old life doesn't fit.

Unwelcome fear reared its head. Even if she yearned to try, what if she failed?

Why hadn't her family known where to find her?

She walked to the window for the umpteenth time tonight and peered into the darkness. Still no James.

Just as well. She doused the lights and climbed into bed.

However unlikely the prospect that she could sleep.

JAMES WAS UP before dawn, though his night had been very short. He tiptoed down the hall to Luisa's kitchen, intending to brew some coffee to surprise her. To thank her for inviting him to sleep in her sewing room, for her help in contacting the owner of the cabin. His head was so full of all he planned to accomplish today before he could be with Bella that noticing the light required a second.

"Buon giorno!" Luisa was bundled into a fluffy robe of an eye-popping electric blue as she placed strips of bacon into a cast-iron skillet. "How many eggs would you like?"

"Two would be great, but you don't have to cook for me. You've already done so much."

"*Pah.* It is nothing." She cast him a glance. "You have, I suspect, much work ahead of you today. You will need the strength."

"I will, indeed." He walked to the coffeepot. "May I pour you a cup?"

She nodded. "You have good manners." She finished arranging the bacon. "What time will your son arrive?"

"About nine, I expect. I want to have the cabin cleaned out before then." He set her cup at her elbow. "Thank you for putting a good word in for me with the owner."

"Raymond kept it for a getaway until recent years, but he can no longer manage the journey. The generous rent you offered will be very welcome." She appeared nearly as scandalized about the price as she had been last night.

James would have paid far more to have a place to spirit away Bella, a refuge for them both. A spot to begin rebuilding their private world without the good doctor glaring at every move James made.

He longed to touch her, to spend hours together, uninterrupted. The very notion that he would be able to make love to her without prying eyes had kept him tossing half the night.

She wasn't ready, he understood that. He wouldn't rush her.

But when she was…they would have a sanctuary.

"That is a dangerous smile," Luisa said, eyes sparkling. "You had better sit down and eat before your mind gets you into trouble."

James laughed, too full of hope and anticipation to resent that his thoughts must be too visible on his face. When Luisa laid the plate before him, he grasped her hand. "Your Romeo was a very lucky man."

Pleasure blossomed on her features, and he could picture the young woman who'd loved so wholly. Then her expression softened, and she squeezed back. "You do love her."

"With every cell in my body." He had to look away. "I came so close to losing her. I couldn't stand it if—"

"Love can endure more than we imagine. Be patient with her, James."

He glanced up. "I'm working at it. I swear I am."

"A little more coffee, then." She patted his hand and picked up his cup. "You do not strike me as a man who gives up easily."

"That I'm not," he said, then felt an unwelcome flutter of nerves. "But what if she never—" He couldn't bring himself to say the words.

"If she falls in love with the man you are now, the past will not matter."

A big *if*. But almost a desired one. A new chance. Free from old mistakes.

And if she did remember…everything?

Please. Let all that we had together, all we could have again, be enough to outweigh my terrible mistake.

CHAPTER FIFTEEN

"Can I go visit her, Dad? I mean, I'm not out to get in your way or make things worse, but—" Bashful, hopeful, leery—all were present in Cameron's expression.

How could James fault his son for wanting exactly what he did—to connect with Bella. To know that she was part of the family again. He clapped Cameron's back. "Of course you can. I'm sure she'd be glad."

"Great! As soon as we get this unloaded, I'll head over."

"I can do that. You go on."

"Really?" Eagerness radiated from him. "Lot of stuff here, Dad. Where will you put it all?"

James found himself oddly reluctant to elaborate on his plans, but he wasn't in the habit of deceiving his children. "I discovered a small cabin up the mountain. A place where your mother and I don't have to be guests."

A slow grin widened. "A love shack, eh?" Cameron appeared both sly and embarrassed. He punched James on the shoulder. "Way to go, Dad."

Except for a few uncomfortable conversations about safe sex and being a considerate lover, James had never discussed his and Bella's love life with his kids. With anyone else, for that matter.

But sometimes you just had to laugh. "O-o-kay. Thanks for the blessing. I think we'll just skip along to another topic now."

Cameron chuckled, too, if a bit nervously. "Amen to that." He paused. "But…good luck, you know? Man, it must be tough, with her not remembering and all." He acted as though the notion had only now occurred to him, which, being a kid, was probably the case. "You sort of have to do the whole business from scratch, like attracting her all over again and first kisses and—" He held up his hands. "Definitely TMI, Dad."

Kidspeak for Too Much Information. "You got that right. Now, why don't you go on and see your mother, and we'll just forget this conversation."

Cam winked. "Sure thing, Dad. But if you want some advice, since you're, like, out of practice after all these years, you just say the word."

"I think the old man will just have to wing it, son. I'll hope that some things are like riding a bicycle— you never completely forget."

Cam grinned. "Well, if you change your mind, the Love Doctor is open for business." He laughed and danced away as James glowered playfully at him.

"Thanks. I'll make sure I've got the number on speed dial," James countered.

His son turned to leave, then halted. "For real,

though, Dad, if there's anything…" Boyish yearning was all over his face.

"I promise it will all work out. We just have to have faith. And patience."

"I wish I could fly you both back with me today." Then youthful high spirits reared again. "But this love-shack thing…you two are long overdue for it."

"Get out of here," James said with pretended gruffness, hijacked by his deep affection. "And not a word to your mother."

Cam drew an imaginary zipper across his lips and loped off toward Bella's quarters.

James finished loading the rented SUV. *Love shack.* He chuckled and headed up the road.

GLOVED HAND on one hip, Bella tapped the trowel against her thigh with the other as she stared at the ground she'd planted with the last of the bulbs.

However hard she attempted to focus on gardening, though, she could not seem to wrest her mind from the topic that was absorbing far more of her mind.

James Parker. Who still hadn't shown.

Maybe he'd changed his mind. Decided that she was too much work. Too much trouble.

She hurled the trowel to the ground. Well, if he had, then just too bad. Just too blasted—

Oh, God. What if something was wrong, instead? Her fury evaporated as worry hit her. Maybe something had happened to Cam or Cele. Or James had been in a wreck, going back to—

Where was he staying, come to that?

She whirled to head for Sam's house to talk to Luisa.

And was face-to-face with her son.

"You okay, Mom?" He was beside her in an instant.

She clasped both hands on his cheeks. "What are you doing here?" Suddenly aware that she still wore dirty gloves, she cast them off and brushed at his face. "Is your father okay?"

"He's fine. What's upset you?"

"He's fine?" she echoed. "Then why—" *Isn't he here?* But she clamped her mouth shut before she could complete the question.

"I brought some…things to him." His gaze evaded hers, and she wondered why. "I have to, uh, leave in a little while, but I just…" He shrugged. "I wanted to see you. Is that all right?"

If she never remembered him, he had already secured a place in her heart. "Of course." She stroked his cheek again. "I'm very happy you're here. Do you have time for a cup of tea?"

He grimaced. "I've never understood your tea fixation."

"Fixation?" She smiled. "Huh. Well, don't tell me you like coffee. You know it'll turn—"

"Your knees black," they said in unison.

His grin was huge. "Grandma Parker always says that."

"Is she—" how odd to be asking "—still alive? And James's dad?"

"Grandpa died when I was nine, but Grandma's

still trucking along. She asked Cele and me to stay with her while Dad and you—" He shrugged again and didn't finish.

"What does she look like?" She touched his arm. "Does it bother you for me to ask?"

"It's weird, but no, I don't mind. As a matter of fact, I brought a few things, pictures and stuff, but I couldn't decide if it would be pushy to show you." He paused, hand over his hip pocket, as if waiting for her verdict.

A frisson rippled through her, part anticipation, part fear. One day, something had to be the trigger, the missing key. How would it feel? She'd lost faith that any solution would be simple.

She smiled, as much to reassure herself as him. "I'd like that."

He held out a palm, and she took the proffered envelope, holding her breath as she lifted the flap. For a second, she faltered, desperate for a delay to make tea or…anything.

But the hope in his eyes wouldn't let her.

She drew out several photographs and a folded paper.

Her knees weakened, and she locked them to steady herself.

Cam's arm went around her shoulder. "Let's go sit," he suggested.

Gratefully, she accompanied him to the porch and sank to the steps. "Thank you." He was the oddest mix of callow and thoughtful, eager and shy. Man and boy.

The top photo was unmistakably of Cam, barely

up to her shoulder, standing beside a younger version of herself. They were on a blinding-white beach, laughing and windswept.

"Where is this?"

"Destin. The Parker family has a beach house there. It was my tenth birthday, and you convinced Dad to let me parasail."

"At ten?"

"Yeah. You about had a heart attack, but you knew how bad I wanted it. I'd only been bugging you both since I first watched someone do it when I was about four. You made me wait until I was double digits."

"Double— Oh, ten." She patted her heart. "Was I insane or did you drop something in my tea?" But she smiled.

"Neither. Just the best mom in the world. Someone who always listened to me, who heard what I didn't even know myself sometimes."

She glanced over at him, those dark eyes brimming with emotion, and she felt her own sting. At the honor, at the loss. "Somehow I think I might have been the lucky one."

His tears spilled over, and hers followed. The air was full of sorrow and longing, as much hers as his.

"I'm really trying, Cameron."

He brushed at his eyes. "I know. Please don't worry. I can wait." He pointed at another. "The next is one Cele wanted you to have, even though she lectured me about taking this chance."

Bella swallowed a lump in her throat. "Please

don't walk on eggshells with me. Surely I'm tougher than that."

"You are, Mom, I swear it. You're the strongest woman I ever met. We're just scared."

"I know. Me, too." She sniffed and wiped her cheeks, then moved to the next photo, one of Cele, about seven or eight, dressed in a clown costume that matched Bella's and beaming with pride.

"She wanted to sew, so you let her help stitch her Halloween outfit. You sewed ours from scratch, every single year."

"What sort of costumes?"

"Oh, wow, let me think… I've been a pirate and a Power Ranger, a dinosaur and Neil Armstrong. Cele was the Princess Bride, Wonder Woman, Susan B. Anthony, Jackie Kennedy…"

Bella did a double take. "Susan B. Anthony and Jackie Kennedy? Wasn't Cele a little young for those?"

"What can I say, Mom? Cele's weird. Got this I Am Woman Hear Me Roar thing going."

"Don't poke fun at your sister."

His grin was enormous. "You sound just like a mom."

She quit fighting to remember and, for a moment, simply reveled in the pleasure of sharing laughter with her son.

There were other photos and more stories. Her and the kids at Walt Disney World, mugging for the camera. Him lying flat in a pile of leaves, Cele raining more down on his head.

She traced a finger over their faces. "A happy family."

"The best," Cam said. "All my friends envied me. Everyone said I had the coolest mom around."

The yearning she could hear nearly undid her. She longed to make promises, but Sam's warnings wouldn't leave her.

Then a thought occurred to her. "Why none of your father?"

He flushed a deep red. "Uh, Dad has his own plans."

She waited for him to say more, but when he didn't, she opened the folded piece of paper.

"Kind of a dumb choice, but you still had it on the refrigerator."

It was a drawing, obviously several years old, depicting Cameron Parker, Astronaut, first man to set foot on Mars.

"Isn't college required to become an astronaut?"

"Yes, but—"

"And the military?"

"Well, sure, but—"

She faced him. "So what are you waiting for?"

"Cele's the genius student."

"You're a bright young man, Cameron. What's the problem?"

"My grades aren't the best."

"Could they improve? If this was important enough?"

"Yes, ma'am."

"Well, is it? Are you willing to get serious? Dreams don't just fall into your lap, you know."

"I—I was afraid. Anyhow, I'm flying now."

"Doing extremely well at it, your father tells me."

"But what if I fail?"

"What if I never get my memory back?"

His eyes widened.

She stuck out her hand. "A deal, then. I don't get discouraged about regaining my memory, and you work as hard in school as you do in the wild blue yonder. And you check out ROTC."

He hesitated.

She arched one eyebrow. "Chicken?"

Cam laughed. "If we spit on our palms first, it's more binding."

"You must think I was born yesterday."

They laughed and shook hands.

HE'D INTENDED to be done before lunch, but the cabin had been full of cobwebs and mouse droppings he had to clear before he could install what he'd brought. Then he'd had to shower, and Luisa had insisted he must have a bite to eat before he went to Bella.

The only real hunger he felt, though, was for her. He could scent her on the bedding Cam had brought from their room at home, could remember her slender fingers plucking the strings of her guitar. Not since he'd been a boy had he had such a case of raging hormones.

Or an attack of nerves of this magnitude.

He paused before her door, surprised not to find her outside in the crisp sunshine. Thunderheads were building to the north, but he'd checked the weather with Luisa, and she'd said they'd have time to make it to the cabin and back before dark without the predicted storm interfering.

There was no room to delay, however, so he took a deep breath and knocked.

Pleasure, surprise—and slight pique—scampered over her features. "Hello," Bella said.

"Hi."

They might as well be thirteen and attending a junior-high dance.

"Did you see Cam?"

"I had a lovely visit—" she said at the same moment.

Awkward smiles. Mutual hesitation.

"You first," he offered.

But she didn't speak, and her scrutiny had him wondering if he measured up. He couldn't say he liked it.

"I didn't ask if this was a bad time."

She shook her head. Bit her lip.

"What is it?" he asked.

"I thought you'd be here this morning." Her tone aimed for neutral but fell short. "Not that you made any promises," she said hastily. "Or that you owe me anything."

His heart skipped. She'd missed him. "I was working on a surprise for you."

"The pictures? Cam said you had some to show me."

"I'd like to show you more than that." He held out a hand. "Will you accompany me?"

"Where?"

"It wouldn't be a surprise if I told you."

She smiled. "Should I wear anything special? Bring something?"

Wear nothing at all, he'd like to say. Instead, he pulled something out of the bag he'd stashed by the door. "I had Cam bring your ski jacket." He hoped she'd recognize it, a rich, deep purple lined with turquoise, an excellent foil for her black hair.

She made a sound of pleasure as she reached for it, and for a moment his spirits lifted.

"It's gorgeous." There was only delight in her voice, not familiarity.

James cautioned himself that he was in for heartache if he pinned too much on each item. The point was to form a bond now, not dwell in the past.

"Thanks. I bought it for you a couple of years ago in Aspen."

"I ski?"

"You like hot chocolate in the lodge better." He grinned.

"How about you?"

He shrugged. "Cam and I have to go do our manly thing every winter possible. He's getting better than me, hard as it is to admit."

"He's young."

"And I'm not, is your point." He held up a hand

at her protest. "No, it's true. I'm growing older. Slowing down."

"You look good to me," she said.

His gaze locked on hers. "Thank you." The ensuing silence buzzed with all he'd like to say.

But wouldn't. Instead, he gestured behind him. "Ready?"

Her pupils nearly swallowed the green of her irises, but she nodded and closed the door behind her.

ON THE DRIVE, Bella found herself mute in his presence, partly from anticipation, some from worry. Cam had been so excited about James's surprise that she was unsettled. What could it be? What if she didn't like it?

What did he expect from her, and would she respond correctly?

Then James removed one hand from the steering wheel and covered hers. "You seem worried. This is supposed to be fun."

She summoned a smile for him. "It will be. I just—" She shook her head and glanced away.

"What?" His voice was kind. Caring.

"I don't—" She gnawed at her lip. "I don't want to disappoint you."

He drew her fingers to his mouth, and the warm breath of him seeped into her skin. "This isn't a test, Bella." He put on the brake, then faced her, still gripping her hand. Pressed a kiss to it. "We're both feeling our way through. There's no right or wrong. I have as much to prove as you, maybe more."

"Why do you say that?"

"I have to convince you that I'm worth what you'd be risking. You have the chance to begin afresh, be who and what and where you want. My task is to entice you to fall in love with me when I don't have the benefit of a young body or a clean slate to offer you. I have baggage I can't abandon, and you may not wish to accept any of it."

His perspective staggered her. "James, I don't have any money or a way to support myself. I can't just begin a new life."

"Of course you can. Bella, did you think I'd just abandon you, even if you didn't want me? You're a bright, strong, beautiful woman who would probably do just fine without me, but even if that's your choice, you're entitled to half of everything we own. I'll support you until you figure out what your heart desires." His eyes were stark with longing. "But I'm hoping you'll decide that's me."

"You would do that?" Her mind was racing. "Let me choose my path?"

His expression was bleak. "I love you, Bella. I won't force you to stay with me. I certainly won't use money to hold you hostage." He shifted on the seat. Started the engine and put it in Reverse.

She realized he was going to drive her to Sam's. "Wait." She placed one hand on his arm. "What about my surprise?"

"It was a fool's errand."

Somehow, she'd tainted the mood. When he'd

arrived today, there had been an air of suppressed excitement about him, but it had evaporated.

"James." When he didn't respond, she said his name again. "James, look at me."

His jaw was tight, his gaze shuttered.

"This is hard, isn't it? I feel all thumbs. Unsure what to say or feel, how to act. I'm so lost, but it never occurred to me that you might be uneasy, too. You always seem so confident, and I can tell from the way the kids behave that it's nothing new." He was listening, she sensed, and she desperately wished they could return to the point where they were holding hands and the anticipation sizzled.

"You might not want me anymore—have you considered that? If I never remember, maybe the Bella you'd wind up with wouldn't be the one you loved. It goes both ways. I'm not going to bind you to promises you made to another woman, one I may never be again."

He shut off the engine. Gripped her shoulders, his gaze fierce. "I will love you until the day I die, Bella Parker." Then his mouth seized hers, hot and rushed at first, gentling to sweet and slow and wicked.

She welcomed the chance to fall into the spell and linger.

But seconds later, he pulled away and stared into her eyes for a long time, then stroked her cheek.

And let her go. "There's a storm on the way. We have to leave now or wait for another day." His voice told her clearly what he wished but that the decision was hers.

Shell-shocked from the tumult erupting inside her, Bella could barely summon a coherent thought.

Except that she wasn't yet ready to part from the complicated man beside her. "I want my surprise," she said.

His slashing grin could have fit a buccaneer. "One surprise coming up."

CHAPTER SIXTEEN

MINUTES LATER, he stopped the car again, but this time he emerged from his seat and walked around to her door, then opened it. "We have a little hike from here."

She started to climb down, but he didn't budge. Instead, he lifted her with impressive ease and lowered her to her feet. When she touched ground, he still didn't move, nor did he speak. Only scoured her features for the longest time...until finally, he picked up one lock of her hair, brushed it over his lips...and retreated.

When he held out his hand for hers, she waited for her pulse to steady, but it was a losing cause. She placed her fingers in his and followed his lead. Along the path, she paid little attention to her surroundings, certain deep within that with him, she was safe. Correction: not safe—too stirred up for that—but in good hands. Protected from everything—

Except temptation.

Long legs led the way. Broad shoulders carved a path. He held branches aside, helped her over a log. His actions could have been interpreted as courtesy.

Except that around them the air swirled thick with desire.

Okay, so sue me. The man makes me hot. She had the urge to cast away all considerations but the hum within her, the crackling air between them.

He was her husband. They would be doing nothing wrong. But some inner voice spoke caution, that the barrier, once crossed, would be final.

He was a stranger, less so each day but still largely unknown.

If only she were positive she was ready.

He glanced over his shoulder. "Problem?" In his gaze, she saw hope and dread.

I won't force you.

At some point, she had to begin believing him.

"No." She smiled and sought to convince him.

As well as herself.

SHE WAS A HALF STEP from running away like a frightened doe, James thought as they reached the clearing. She didn't lie worth a damn.

"Oh, look!" she said. "It's lovely. Whose is it?"

She certainly wasn't hard to please. The shack was barely habitable. "Ours, at least for now."

"What do you mean?"

He faced her. "I leased it from the owner. I wanted a place for us to be alone." He waited for her to tense.

When instead she smiled and arched one eyebrow, he knew his Bella was still alive and kicking. "Really." She cut him a glance. "You devil."

The phrase stole his breath. She'd called him that a thousand times. Ten thousand. When she was flirting.

He didn't remark on it, though. From second to second, they walked a tightrope. He was tired of falling off. "Let's go inside." He opened the door, held it wide. "After you, madam." He swept her a courtly bow.

She grinned and curtsied. "Why, thank you, sir." Said as *suh*...honey and cream, Southern and slow. The voice of the siren he'd lost somewhere down the years.

He followed her in. She halted just inside the door. A part of him lingered, waiting for her reaction to the items that Cam had delivered.

She trailed her fingers over the quilt she'd pieced so long ago, and paused. That quilt—her own design, a stunning watercolor in cascading shades of blues, greens and bronzes—had topped their bed from the second year of their marriage until not long after Bella began selling real estate.

And had a decorator redo their room.

Their room. Their refuge. The spot where they'd slept and fought, played and laughed and moaned in bliss.

But she moved on without comment, and he couldn't help feeling the disappointment. *You created that,* he wanted to tell her. *You provided every speck of color that graced my life.*

Instead, he remained silent.

She spotted the rocking chair he'd made for her. "Yours?" she asked as she stroked the wood.

"Yours." He gestured for her to sit.

She walked around it, then spied the guitar and uttered a small gasp.

His heart kicked up.

"Sam said I might have played guitar."

James was sick of hearing *Sam said*, but he smiled. "You did."

She hesitated. "Did, not *do?*"

"You've been busy with your career."

She frowned, then picked up the guitar and settled on the front of the rocking chair. Tentatively, she strummed across the strings.

Smiled at the sound.

James watched her, head bent as he'd so often seen it. *Play,* he urged silently. *Play for me.*

She plucked one note, then two. Tightened a string and plucked the strings in sequence.

Instinctively tuning it. Hope rose.

Then Bella began to play, hesitantly at first, but soon with confidence. A note missed here and there; still, her fingers flew. "Greensleeves," "Let It Be," then—

Oh, God. James faced away as Bella launched into a song she'd composed just for him. It had no lyrics, as far as he was aware, and had never been written down. As he considered how close he'd been to never hearing it again, he realized he had to get Bella to record it. She hummed the melody in that husky contralto voice of hers, and James busied himself building a fire, so she couldn't tell how much hearing her destroyed him.

He didn't want her to stop; he couldn't bear it if,

at the end of this devastating journey to the heart of who they were, she still viewed him as a stranger. He longed to believe that when she finished playing, she would be the Bella he'd loved for most of his life.

He was scared to death that she would not.

Please. He'd gone rusty at praying until Bella had disappeared; now it seemed that was all he did, beg for mercy and wish for grace he didn't deserve. *I've done her wrong, but please, please...let me have another chance.*

The music stopped then.

James froze right where he was.

THE NOTES DIED AWAY, and Bella emerged slowly from the dream. A fire was glowing merrily, removing the chill. Her gaze snagged on that quilt and, shutter-quick, she caught the faintest outlines of an image.

She was sitting on the quilt, playing the song she'd just finished. Her hair kept getting in the way, and she shook it back over her shoulder.

A finger traced over her flesh, and she felt warmth behind her. A body. Skin.

James.

She hugged the guitar to her chest. "Have I—" She had to clear her throat. "Have I played this for you before, on...on that quilt?"

He stirred then. "Yes."

"James, I— Just for a second, I thought—" Why wouldn't he face her? "Are you all right?"

"Yeah. Sure." He sounded anything but.

She propped the guitar against the wall and rose. Made her way to him and knelt. "James." She placed one hand on his knee. "Tell me about the first time we made love."

He didn't speak for a moment, then, "You were fearless."

"Me?"

At last, he met her eyes. "Yes."

His expression was so serious that she changed her mind. "You don't have to discuss it if you don't want to."

"You were playful and sweet and insanely sexy—" He stood abruptly. "I can't do this." He crossed the room. Shoved his hands in his pockets and stared outside.

"What's wrong?"

"Nothing. I just—" He shook his head. "I hoped that maybe if you saw—" he gestured around the room "—all of this, you'd recall."

"I'm sorry."

"Not your fault."

"It absolutely is."

"No—" He kicked a chair, sent it skidding. "It's not. I'm to blame for letting you leave. For you being where that bastard could hurt you. I'd like to kill him with my bare hands." He slammed his fist into the door, his body rigid, his chest heaving with the power of his fury. This was a James she had not met.

She wasn't afraid of him, though. She'd learned him that well. She went to him and wrapped her arms around his rib cage. "I'm all right, James. Shh. It's all going to be okay, I promise." She soothed him with words, with her tone…

With a kiss to the corner of his mouth.

Fury snapped with an audible crack, and hunger seized control. James crushed her against him, no more the hesitant suitor, the patient, grieving man. This was primal, elemental…a man claiming his mate.

Just as suddenly, he jolted away from her. "I'm sorry."

Wheeled and strode outside.

"James—"

He made it to the edge of the clearing. He was quivering like a stallion primed to charge into battle—

Or to breed. To cover. Bella had the fleeting thought that she should be shocked or frightened.

Instead, she was electrified. Someone new assumed the place of the woman who'd felt so lost, so afraid. Perhaps she should exercise caution, wait for him to make the next move.

No. This new woman tossed her head…

And followed.

He heard her approach. "Stay where you are." His tone was clipped. "Get your coat. We're leaving."

She smiled. "Make me."

He whipped around, eyes narrowed. "What did you just say?"

"You heard me." When his expression reflected his confusion, laced with the last traces of anger, she seized the moment. "You know what? I'm sick of being *poor*

Bella. It's getting on my nerves. Aren't you tired of treating me like I'm going to shatter any second?"

"You've been through a lot," he said with caution.

"I have, but I'm beginning to realize that you may have been through just as much." When he blinked as though she'd lost her mind, she took heart. Closed the distance between them and laid her hand on his cheek. "You seem so weary. Come back inside with me," she cajoled. "Let's sit by the fire. You can lay your head in my lap." She cast him a saucy smile. "Maybe you'll decide it would be fun to make out." She began to walk back.

He grabbed her in one step. Spun her back to him. "I'm not dead yet, sweetpea." Then his mouth was on hers, and she wasn't sure who moaned.

But she suspected it might be her.

Oddly free and delighted by her own daring, she danced from his grasp and raced to the house.

He caught her up and threw her over his shoulder. She giggled helplessly as he carried her inside.

Once the door was shut, he lowered her down the front of his body with exquisite slowness, pausing once or twice to apply his lips at a tender spot.

And she melted. Just…melted. "James…"

"Bella, oh, Bella," he murmured as his lips cruised her body. "Let me have you, baby. Please, let me love you."

"Yes," she whispered from a throat hoarse with longing, sinking her fingers into his hair. "Oh, yes."

He scooped her up and strode to the bed, where

he laid her on the quilt as though she were made of crystal. Their hands tangled as they tore away clothes, first hers, then his.

He leaned over her, one knee beside her hip, and let his gaze range at will, his eyes laser hot. "You are the most beautiful woman I've ever seen."

Doubt blindsided her. She wasn't young. She didn't really know him. She scrabbled at the covers, tried to conceal herself.

"Don't," he said. "Please."

But she was painfully aware that she was naked. "I just—"

Sorrow crept over his features. Loneliness. He began to back away. "I…get it. This all feels so familiar to me, like coming home at last. But for you, it's— I'm—" He averted his head. "A stranger."

Bella sought to understand her whipsaw emotions. As he reached for his jeans, she grasped for his wrist. "Don't go."

He shook his head. "You're not ready. It would be wrong."

She wrapped the quilt around her torso and walked to his side. "James, look at me."

"No." Sharp. Pain-filled. But at last he complied. "I'm sorry. This is just so damn lonely."

She witnessed the toll on him—love warring with loneliness, longing vying with caution, and over it all, a haze of deep unhappiness. "I wish it would happen, that click of the key in the lock. I can't tell you how much."

"No—don't put that pressure on yourself. I never meant to. It was only that having you taunt me, flirt with me, was so much like when we first met." His eyes glittered. "The girl I fell in love with the first day." He faced her. "But I love more than that girl. I love all the women you've been, the wife, the mother, the lover, the gardener…" Carefully, he cupped her face in his hands and pressed a resigned kiss to her forehead. "I'll wait, Bella. However long is required."

She could feel him leaving her even as he stood only inches away, and something in her became more angry than frightened. So much had been stolen from them.

"No." She lifted her head. Gripped his wrists. "I'm tired of careful. I'm sick of being at the mercy of fate." She put her heart into her words, her expression. "You and Cele and Cam have suffered just as much, and I won't sit by idly, not one more second, do you hear me?"

Frowning, he caressed her jaw with one finger. "What are you saying?"

"That I want you to make love with me. Not to me, you hear? *With* me. Maybe I don't remember how it was, but that doesn't mean we can't create our own new relationship, does it?" She stood on tiptoe to reinforce her point. "Let's take back our lives, James. Starting here. Now."

Fervently, she put her mouth on his. Swiped her tongue across his lips until he opened them.

Flush with a sense of control for the first time since she'd awakened, she all but pounced. Threw her arms around his neck, let the quilt fall and pressed her skin to his.

Then swiveled her hips over his groin to make her point.

All his hesitation vanished.

The dance they began was not a smooth waltz or a lazy samba. She'd have thought his moves would be practiced, but when she felt him tremble, she understood that he was as nervous as she beneath her bravado.

She didn't have to remember him to love him then.

James drew her to the bed. Touched her as if she were a miracle, and she responded in kind. He grew bolder, using his body and her own to devastating effect.

Their fractured tango turned torrid. Not flawless, at moments graceless—but powered by pain and hope, need and fear and a beauty surprising in its strength.

Somewhere along the way, she stopped thinking, ceased inventorying her reactions and creeping carefully to find her path.

Instead, she gloried in his touch, his taste, surrendered to the dizzying pleasure. When she seized the initiative, shoved him over and mounted, his fierce expression softened to a fond smile, as if this behavior was a facet of who she really was.

She threw her head back in abandon and heard James laugh from sheer delight.

His hands raked her hair, slid to her hips, coaxed her higher. Clever fingers and skillful mouth sent her reeling, then she was gone and gone and—

She bent to him. "Come with me." Sealed her mouth to his.

He growled, flipped her to her back and joined them. Bella gasped, and for a second, she lost the ability to breathe.

Then she soared once more, this time caught with him in a bliss like one pure note of music. For brief, unbearably precious moments, they were no longer strangers, despite everything that had sundered them.

Simply...James. His Bella.

One.

CHAPTER SEVENTEEN

THUNDER RUMBLED in the distance.

James opened his eyes but didn't move.

Bella lay beside him at last, legs tangled with his, her breathing the sweetest melody he'd ever heard. His arms tightened instinctively to keep her there, and she stirred.

He buried his face in the tumble of her curls and prayed for her not to awaken.

He wasn't ready. He had no idea what to say. How to hold to his promise when being so near her, being inside her, had been better than any memory, any dream.

You know me, he said silently. *Deep within, far past consciousness, you sense that we belong.*

But the shadow over his joy was his betrayal, inexplicable as it was, then and now.

As he rediscovered Bella, he was hauntingly aware of how they'd taken their nearly magical connection too much for granted. They belonged together in the most primal way, but they'd allowed their attention to fragment. Focused too much on

their children and their other responsibilities and
assumed that their bond would hold, that it didn't
require tending.

Even the strongest link, he realized, could grow
rusty and weaken if not maintained. As the economic
pressures on the company had grown, he'd put more
and more hours into saving it. He hadn't compre-
hended how much Bella had lost her bearings when
the children had left home, and he'd considered her
urging him to take time off as a distraction, a luxury.
Something to be dealt with later.

He hadn't explained. Hadn't wanted to talk about
his troubles when he spent all day wrestling with
them. Had, he understood now, shut Bella out in the
name of shielding her.

So she had found a new focus that required many
hours away from the home that was too empty—and
their time together had become even more scarce.

Here was a second chance for them.

Typically, it was Bella who had made the first
leap into the unknown.

It was good, so very good, to be with her again.
If she never remembered, he thought it would be
okay, after all. She already cared about the kids, and
if she'd felt a fraction of the power he had just now,
there was reason for optimism. They could make a
life, perhaps an even better one.

The temptation to keep silent about why they'd
parted was strong. He would not stray again, no
question. Bella would never have to know, and how

would he explain it when she had no context? It hadn't been about sex, anyway—he'd been too proud to tell Bella how bad the company's situation was and thus had robbed them both of the chance to fight it together. He'd fallen for an understanding ear, a respite, and that one fall from grace had left the taste of ashes in his mouth.

But he'd never lied to Bella before, not about anything more serious than a surprise.

He craved a clean slate, an honest start. He only needed a little more time to cement what they'd begun tonight, then he would tell her. And pray that she would find enough good in him to make her want to forgive him.

He would never forgive himself. Or settle until they were past it.

Please, he beseeched. *She is my heart.* He embraced her, clasped treasured curls in one fist. "I love you," he whispered.

"Hmm." Bella sighed. Wriggled closer without opening her eyes. "Mmm…"

She squirmed against him, and his body responded.

You don't have to forgive me, he promised silently as he rolled her to her back. Moved over her. *I'll earn your love again, I swear.* He slipped between her legs, put his mouth to her throat. *Just don't leave me, my love.*

He grazed her body with kisses, fastened his lips to one breast.

She jolted as though someone had thrown a breaker and sent electricity racing through her. "James?"

"I'm here. I'll always be here."

And he set out to bind them once more.

"IT'S RAINING," she said lazily, stroking his head where it rested, pillowed between her breasts.

"Yeah."

"You don't sound worried that we could get stuck here."

He lifted his head. Met her smile. "It'd be a real shame."

"Indeed."

He swirled his tongue over her nipple.

She arched her back. Felt his body respond. "Aren't we supposed to be too old to do it this often?"

"We've got time to make up for." He chuckled. "Anyway, there are worse ways to die." He sat up. "You're right, though. The spirit's willing, but I'd hate for you to have to drag my cold, dead body down this mountain." He stood. "You hungry?"

"Starving."

Abruptly, he sank back and dragged her into his lap. Cradled her near. "I've missed this so much, just holding you. Do you mind?"

His cheek rested on her head. "Uh-uh." She snuggled close, feeling both oddly naked and absolutely comfortable. Cherished.

Falling in love with this man would be no challenge. She was halfway there already.

Then he tensed. "Bella, I should tell you—"

A massive crack of thunder shook the entire cabin.

James gripped her, then released her. "Wow. I'd better bring in some more wood. I don't think we're leaving just yet." He shoved his legs into his pants and began to dress. "Don't be frightened. We're not at the peak, and there are much higher trees to attract the lightning."

She grinned. "I'm not the least bit afraid with you."

His expression was hard to interpret in the increasing shadows. "You can count on me, Bella, I swear it. I will always take care of you."

Then he shrugged on his coat and was out the door.

Sighing, drifting, Bella did a little pirouette. And laughed for sheer, lazy, ridiculous joy.

Then she donned her clothing, too, and went to figure out what she could fix for them to eat.

"YOU THOUGHT AHEAD," she teased as they devoured the soup she'd heated, the dark bread she had made the day before with Luisa. "Are you always such a planner?"

"Guilty as charged." He smiled, but she could feel the reservation in him, a small indefinable space that had crept between them.

After what they'd shared, she'd been ready to cast her lot with him, let him transport her wherever was home. They had been one, she would swear it, one heart, one soul as two bodies joined.

But now...a subtle distance was making her uneasy again.

Would they ever be completely comfortable with each other?

Time for another step. "James?"

"Hmm?" He broke from his preoccupation.

"Cameron said you have pictures."

"Maybe you've had enough for one day."

She placed her hand on his arm. "What's wrong?" Then she removed it. "Maybe you regret—" She withdrew into herself.

He shoved back his chair. Knelt beside hers and clasped her hands. "Never. Not for one second." His expression was intent. "It was everything to me. *You* are everything, Bella. My life, all the joy and beauty I've ever known." His voice roughened. "You changed me." He glanced away. "But I'm afraid I changed you more."

He was so obviously upset. "What do you mean?" To soothe him, though, she brushed her fingers over his hair.

He rose to pace. "You were never meant to be caged. You're a butterfly, a rare one, with a value beyond price." He locked his eyes on hers. "From the moment I met you, my world held colors I'd never seen. Riches I couldn't imagine."

She could only shake her head. "I don't feel rare."

"And that's my shame. As much as I've loved you—and I have, Bella, with every breath—" He neared her again. "I trapped you. Our lives became too much like the world I was from, not the dreams you had for us."

"I don't understand." His intensity had her wishing for some room to breathe.

"I—" He spread his fingers. "It would be a long story, but maybe the pictures will help. Let me show you what you were. What happened to us."

"I was unhappy with you?"

"I don't know. I didn't think you were, but I was busy, too busy with the company. I missed the signs."

"It's a big responsibility, all those employees."

He brought out a box. Set it on the table. "Don't excuse me, Bella. I don't deserve it."

"People get overloaded, James. Don't be so hard on yourself— Oh, look!" She spied a photo on top. "It's Cam, isn't it? This—" She smiled. "This is the baby I remembered…" Her voice trailed off as she tilted the photo into the light. "Your hand…" Her gaze jerked up to his. "James, this is what I remembered, this picture. Exactly. I drew it one night. I was scared to death I'd forget it again. This is what convinced me to override Sam and get my photo put out for the world to see." She clenched his arm. "I wanted my family. I could feel Cam's hair, how it was to have your arm around us both, and I wanted that."

She could barely see him through eyes swimming with tears. "I've been so lonely. So lost. Oh, James…" She leaned into him, needing his embrace, his strength. The assurance that she wasn't adrift anymore, that she belonged.

When he enfolded her and bent his head to hers, rocking her slowly, for the first time since she'd awakened, she began to truly believe that the nightmare would be over.

"I can love you, James. I want to. I'll try harder to remember—"

He clutched her so tightly she could barely breathe. "Oh, Bella. God—" Agony was in his voice. "I don't deserve you. I've made mistakes. Such mistakes."

"Shh," she murmured, sliding one hand to his cheek. "I'm sure I did, too. We're human, after all." She smiled. "Let me have more pictures. I want to know everything. The house—" She glanced back over her shoulder as she reached for the next one. "Do you have it? I'd like to see where we live."

"Bella—"

"Hush, now. We're together. That's what matters, isn't it?" She picked up an album. "Is it in here?"

He was regarding her as if she were an oasis and he the one lost. "You're my miracle, Bella. Don't ever forget that. Please." So earnest and intent. "And if you'll let me, I'll spend the rest of my life making you happy, completely happy."

How could she not be touched to her marrow? Didn't every woman dream of a man speaking his heart to her? Pledging his soul?

"Let's start here," she said gently. "Show me our home, James. Introduce me to the girl you loved and the boy you were. Let me view how our lives played out." She held the album out to him. "Is this a good place to begin?"

He stiffened, then exhaled as if he was relenting. Giving up some battle. "Yeah," he said. "You put that together, so it probably is."

"Here," she said. "Let's sit together and go over what you've brought me."

"Okay," he said finally. "All right."

They settled, side by side, at the old oak table and began.

CHAPTER EIGHTEEN

She was like a kid in her delight, her absorption. "Oh, lordy, would you check out that dress? What was I thinking?" Her eyes were laughing as she glanced up at him.

"You were beautiful. You still are. The most gorgeous woman I've ever laid eyes on."

"Not in this outfit, buddy." She elbowed him in the side. "With that eighties attempt at Farrah Fawcett's hairdo." She gave a dramatic shudder, then abandoned that page for the next.

He couldn't help stroking the tangle of ringlets. "You should always let it have its way. The curls are so...you."

"A mess." But she chuckled.

"My mess." Overcome, he pressed his face to her hair.

When she leaned into him, even as she kept devouring the images of their life together, the closeness, the ease between them, was a gift.

"Oh, check this out. Is this the factory? Cameron's taller than Cele in this one. When did that happen?"

"When he was in sixth grade, actually. Poor mite. She never stood a chance. And he was insufferable, though not so much as when he passed you in height. He'd walk around patting you on the top of the head. 'Hi, shortie,' he'd say to you, and act like he was going to bust his buttons."

She grinned. "But he never got taller than you."

"Hey, a dad needs some advantage when his boy can run rings around him."

She chuckled, then bent to the pictures again. "You are so imposing in a suit." She traced him with one finger. "But jeans seem more natural, some—how." She glanced at the rocking chair, then at him. "I'd like for you to do more of that. It's where your heart is."

"I can't right now."

"The business troubles you. Want to talk about it?"

"It's not a pretty story."

"Life isn't always pretty." She touched the back of his hand lightly. "I can listen, James. Whether or not I can do anything else to help."

As she would have, all along. If only he'd offered her the chance. If they hadn't lost their way.

He had to say it. Couldn't live the lie any longer. "Bella, there's something I have to tell you first."

She frowned. "What is it?"

How he yearned to grab her and never let her go. "First, you must know that you're the only woman I've ever loved. Ever will."

"You're frightening me." She started to withdraw

a little. The album tipped, and a photo fell out. She grasped for it. Caught a glimpse.

Went very still. She brought the snapshot closer. A shudder shook her. The album fell from her grasp to the floor, and she barely blinked.

James caught a glimpse of the photo, and his heart shriveled. A big day at the plant. His administrative staff surrounded him.

Including Julie.

All color drained from Bella's face. She turned to him, her eyes huge with horror. With anguish and the beginnings of fear. Of him.

She shrank from his touch. Began shivering like the last leaf surrounded by barren branches.

"Sweetheart—" he began, and the old argument echoed in his head. *Why, James?*

It meant nothing.

How could you? I have to go.

Something's dying inside me.

"Oh my God," she barely whispered. "Her. You—" She pointed, and the photo trembled in her hand.

"Bella, I swear to you, it—" *Meant nothing.* That argument hadn't swayed her before. Why would it now? "It was a mistake, a bad one, but it wasn't intentional. If you'll let me, I'll spend the rest of my life making it up to you." He went unashamedly to his knees beside her, every atom of him pleading. "Don't give up on us, Bella. I understand what I've done wrong. Where we both—" But he didn't finish. Yes, she'd made mistakes, but the lion's share of guilt was his.

"I...left you." She studied her ring finger. "The thieves didn't get my ring."

"No." He pulled the circle of gold and diamonds from his pocket where it had been, day and night. Held it up to her.

"I removed it myself. When I—" Her expression was a study in devastation. Despair. She let the photograph flutter from her grasp. Let him see that his fate would be the same.

"Bella, don't walk away from us. From what we had. What we could have."

Grief covered her features. "All of this." Dazed. "None of it had to happen."

His jaw clenched. "No. It's my fault, every bit of it." He locked his eyes on hers. "Will you let me explain?"

She didn't look away, but neither did she speak for long seconds while he felt naked and impotent as never before in his life, not even the night she'd left him.

Because now he truly understood what he'd lost. What he would miss the rest of his life. When he hit rock bottom, anger swam to his rescue. Determination. He took one step toward her.

She set her jaw. Her eyes sparked, and she held her ground.

He was astonished to feel the beginnings of a smile.

"What on earth could you possibly find amusing?" Her own fury was rising to displace the devastation.

"I'm not amused." How could he be, with a heart breaking? "But it's good to encounter the woman who'd as soon spit in my eye as give an inch. Who's broken a cabinet's worth of crockery over the course of our life together."

Fire sparked in her eyes. Her fingers twitched as if they longed for something to throw. "How could you?" A growl. A curse. "You bastard. You—"

Then all the fight fled from her, and her frame collapsed in on itself. "You…hurt me, James. Hurt us. Killed my hope that we'd ever find our way—" She buried her face in her hands and sobbed.

He reached for her, and she flinched.

He'd thought he'd hit bottom, but he'd been wrong. Nothing could wound him worse than having the love of his life reject his comfort.

As the instrument of her pain, he'd lost the right to extend it. He wanted to, desperately, nonetheless.

But he was not the answer.

However bitter the knowledge, he had to try once more. "If you remember that, do you recall the rest? How much we loved each other? All the good years, happy years we had? What an incredible family we were?"

"Were," she said dully.

"Are, Bella." He leaned forward. "All that love isn't gone."

But she shook her head over and over, denying him even an inch.

He could deal with her stubbornness, wait her out. They would stay here until she saw reason.

When she sank to the floor, though, back bowed

in despair, he was afraid of what this would do to her health.

Then he knew what he had to do. "I'll return you to him. Sam." Every word was a knife in his chest. *He* should be her refuge.

But he'd forfeited that privilege. "Despite the storm, if I drive slowly, we should make it."

She didn't respond, and everything in him longed for her to refuse.

Finally, she nodded. "All right." Straightened and wiped at her eyes.

However much she loathed him, he despised himself more. With leaden steps, he began preparations to leave.

Silently, she did the same. They might as well have been on opposite sides of the moon.

He stood at the door with his raincoat to put over her to keep her dry. He didn't care, just now, what happened to him. The rest of his life spread out before him, an endless desert.

She paused over the album and retrieved it, closed it gently. Picked up one of the loose photos of their once-happy family and traced each of their faces, even his.

For a second, faint hope fluttered.

Then she set it on the table, facedown.

Turned her back on their past.

And stepped, deliberately, on the photo that had brought everything crashing back.

THE TRIP DOWN the mountain was silent and cold. The anticipation that had accompanied their ascent only hours earlier as dead as the ashes of their love.

Once at the garage apartment, she hesitated, fingers white on the car-door handle. "Go on home, James."

As he heard the finality of her tone, something stirred him from his despair. "Bella, we have to talk about this. We've shared too much to give up."

She retreated into the rain. "Not now," she said, her gaze as anguished as his soul.

"When?" he asked, voice hoarse.

"I don't know." She stood there, getting drenched, and seemed to feel none of the downpour. "I have to think."

"I'll wait for you. I won't leave until—"

"No. You have a business to save. And children who need you."

"None of that matters," he said bitterly. "Nothing but you. I love you."

You should have thought of that before you betrayed me. He waited for her to say it. He'd earned it.

But she only regarded him sadly. "I loved you, too."

He closed his eyes as grief settled into his bones. *Loved.* Past tense.

He opened them, bent forward. "You still can, Bella. We've had so much joy together, and we can have more. Don't throw it all away over what meant nothing."

At last, her eyes sparked again. "If you say that

one more time, I cannot be held responsible for the consequences."

Most sane individuals would find her threat alarming. He was admittedly barely sane just now, after all they'd been through.

But despite everything, his heart lifted, just a little.

If she was angry, she wasn't indifferent.

"I'm not going anywhere, Bella." When her jaw set, he elaborated. "I'll leave you alone, but I am not running home like a whipped dog." He gentled his voice. "Go on, get inside. You're soaked."

She seemed ready to argue, then changed her mind and walked away.

He watched her through the downpour, and rolled down the window, shouting to be heard. "I may be one stupid son of a bitch, Isabella Rosaline, but I am also a man in love who understands what he's lost. I am going to fight for you. Just you wait."

Then, though he wanted badly to follow her inside and make certain she was dry and warm and safe, he forced himself to throw the vehicle into Reverse and drive off.

But then he saw, in his rearview mirror, Dr. Sam the Opportunist sprinting from his house toward her apartment.

All control vanished. He jammed on the brakes and whipped a U-turn. Closed the gap in seconds and charged from his vehicle, not even bothering to shut the door. Rain was the least of his worries. "Get away from there," he shouted.

Lincoln paused. "What have you done to her?" He swiveled back. "Jane, are you all right? Let me in. Did he hurt you?"

"She's not Jane." A haze of rage dropped over James's vision. "You got that?" He grabbed Lincoln's shoulder and whipped him around. "She's my wife, not yours. Leave her alone."

Lincoln tried to shrug him off, but James could not be moved. He was fighting for his life, his love.

"Jane!" Lincoln shouted. "Tell me you're okay."

When she still didn't answer, the mild-mannered doctor vanished. He grasped for the doorknob.

James lost it. Jerked the man back and slammed a fist into his face.

Lincoln came up swinging. They lost footing in the mud, but Lincoln didn't seem to care, and James sure didn't. He hadn't taken a punch in too many years to count, but his helplessness to sway Bella was swallowed up by the welcome heat of battle. Here was something he could do—beat the hell out of the guy who wanted to steal her from him.

The one she trusted instead of him.

Lincoln landed a good one, and James went down on his back. Just as quickly, he lunged and brought his opponent to the ground with him. They rolled and punched and grunted, but neither man yielded. Lincoln probably had fifteen years on him, and James would feel it later, but in this instant, all he could register was that he was fighting for Bella.

For the life he'd let slip away.

Not one more bit would escape from his grasp, he thought, and reared over the other man, fist drawn back—

"Stop it!" Bella cried. "Both of you!" She waded into the middle.

James shifted to keep her out of harm's way—

And Lincoln caught him square on the chin.

James dropped like a rock.

WHEN HE AWOKE, his body was a mass of sore muscles and bruises. He wrinkled his forehead, winced at a tightness and realized his head had been bandaged. His lip was split, and his right hand was swathed in bandages, too.

He glanced around the strange room that he thought might be part of Lincoln's house. He levered up—

And groaned. Hard. Tomorrow would be a bitch.

Then he recalled Bella rushing into the fray and his attempt to save her.

"Bella?" He scanned the room frantically for a sight of her. "Bella, where are you?" No answer, so he made his way painfully to his feet.

As he trudged toward the door, he heard raised voices.

"Do not phone the sheriff, Sam. Let James be."

"Jane, it's not for my sake—it's for yours. I can tell that he hurt you somehow, even if you won't explain."

"I told you to call me Isabella. And this isn't your business, Sam. This is between us."

Isabella. Heartened, James made his way down
the hall and into the kitchen, where they stood.

But if he'd thought he'd get a welcome from her,
he'd been wrong. "What are you doing up?" Her
tone was frigid.

Lincoln picked up the phone and dialed.

"Sam, no—" Bella grabbed for the receiver.

"Let him," James said. "I'm not afraid of him."

"You should be, you bastard," said Lincoln, and
wheeled on him.

"Bring it on."

"Stop it!" As before, Bella jumped in between
them. "Both of you." She poked James in the chest
and did the same to Lincoln.

James refused to quit glaring at Lincoln.

Until he noticed tears in her eyes. "Sweetheart—"
He moved toward her.

She held out a palm. "Get away from me. You,
too," she said to Lincoln. "Just—just leave me alone.
I'm sick to death of—" Her voice broke, and she ran.

James wanted desperately to follow, but he forced
himself to stay. When Lincoln moved, James grabbed
his shoulder. "Don't. If you care about her, don't
make it worse."

"What did you do to her?"

"Too much to forgive," James answered. And with
that, his hopes faded. He headed for the door. Lincoln
tried to prevent him, and James shook him off. "I'm
not going to her, much as I'd sell my soul for her to
wish for me to." He faced the man whose record with

her was a clean slate. "You intend to move in on her the second you find an opening. I understand that. She's the most amazing woman in the world." He reached to rake his fingers through his hair and winced. "But I'm asking you to give her room. She may not want me anymore, and I can't blame her. I've loved her with everything in me, but I've also wronged her. Taken what we had for granted. She's been through a lot—"

The anguish of knowing she wouldn't seek comfort from him, that his offer of it would be rejected again, was killing him. Of all the things he couldn't bear, leaving Bella alone and wounded hurt him worse than anything he'd ever experienced. "I'm asking you, for her sake, not mine." He met the other man's eyes. "If she decides you're better for her than me, I love her enough to let her go, even though I'd rather someone just put a bullet in me. But if you ever hurt her, there will not be a place on this earth for you to hide."

"I feel the same." The light of battle flared again.

"Then we understand each other," James said grimly. He walked to the backdoor and paused, his gaze fastened on the glow in the window that might as well be a universe away.

CHAPTER NINETEEN

A FAINT KNOCK at the door had Bella stirring. "Go away," she said, and buried her face in the covers.

"It is afternoon," said Luisa. "I have food for you."

She had no interest in talking to anyone. She didn't even want to think. She'd spent hours going around in circles last night, trying to sort out all that had fallen in on her like some collapsing ceiling. "I'm not really hungry," she said to the woman who only meant to be kind.

"Hiding will do you no good, you know. However long you wait."

Bella sighed. And smiled a little. She'd learned enough to understand that Luisa was relentless when she had her mind set on something. "All right, I'm coming." As she emerged, her gaze settled on the wet pile of clothes, garments that had accompanied her through sweaty, beautiful sex, through heartbreaking discovery, through mud-stained battle and tear-drenched bandaging.

And maybe through the end of a marriage.

She yanked open the door, desperate to think of anything but James. "I'm not up for company."

"I really don't care." Luisa smiled at her, both challenge and sweetness.

Bella couldn't help smiling back. Then bursting into tears.

"Oh, child." The much smaller woman embraced her as though their sizes were reversed. "That's right," she soothed. "Cry it out."

Bella did, a storm of weeping that seemed endless. Finally, empty and hopeless, she collapsed on the bed and held her head in her hands. "I don't know what to do."

"What is it you wish for?" Luisa stroked her hair.

She could only shake her head as the jumble of thoughts threatened to overwhelm her again. "To hate him," she whispered. "And not to know what he did. To believe in what we once had."

"Balance is everything, *cara*. In a long marriage, there are peaks and valleys. You understand this, in your heart you do."

"This is no valley. This is the depths of hell."

"Is it?"

Bella's head jerked up. "He betrayed me. He cheated on me. Made a mockery of our life."

"Shh. I am not excusing him. What he did was wrong. But does it negate everything between you? If you tallied up the pluses and minuses, even this gigantic one, are you so certain how they would weigh out?" She paused. "And what if he did the same? Can you say that you played no part in where you two found yourselves?"

In that instant, she would have liked to lash out at Luisa, to point to all the ways in which *she* was clearly the injured party. What he had done was wrong, completely wrong. Unforgivable.

"I don't wish to speak to him now. Maybe ever."

"You could not, even if you liked. He is gone."

"Gone? Where?"

"I have no idea. He left in the night."

"He went home," she said. "To Alabama, like I told him to." Even though he'd said he would fight for her.

"I wonder. Your daughter called here, seeking him because he did not answer his cell phone."

A dart of worry speared into her misery. "What is he playing at? He won't get my attention like this."

"I do not think a man with a broken heart plays games."

Regardless of the state of his heart, James did not play—at anything. Luisa was right about that. The only times he relaxed were when she coaxed him into it. He was always so serious, so responsible.

I believe too many people depend on him, she'd told Sam. *I suspect he doesn't allow himself to think about what he wants because he's so busy taking care of others.*

He hadn't asked to be excused for being worried about the fate of the company and missing the signs that they'd been in trouble.

And she hadn't been there for him, too swallowed up in her grieving over her babies flying the nest.

She'd accused him of being too busy to pay attention to her, but in fact, she'd done the same.

She understood, better than anyone, what a worrier James was. How readily he shouldered burdens, no matter his own needs.

He was a protector, a guardian. The one everyone turned to.

Including her.

And when he'd been alone with his worries, she'd been too caught up in her own sorrow to notice.

Another woman had.

He shouldn't have faltered. Ought to have run, far and fast, back to her. Demanded that she not rush to judgment.

But that was not James. He was a giver. She was the one who made demands. She had the temper; he possessed the patience.

Yet he'd hurt her. So badly. And lied about it.

Then she recalled all the times since he'd been in Colorado that he'd seemed so sad. Appeared to be battling himself. Had started to say something. *Bella, I should tell you—*

"Too late," she said.

"Is it? When there is true love, is it ever too late?" Luisa asked. "Look at me, Bella."

She didn't want to. Her head was spinning with turmoil.

"I said, look at me." Luisa grasped her chin with a tone that brooked no nonsense. "Has he ever done such a thing before?"

Rebelliously, Bella raised her eyes. "No."

"You are angry, but so am I. Do you have a clue what I would do for one more second with my Romeo? Any idea what I would forgive rather than lose him?"

"He didn't cheat on you," she said hotly.

"Did he not?"

Bella gasped. Grabbed her wrist. "Tell me. How you could forgive him. If you did."

"Do not be such a child." Luisa's tone was scathing. "Do you think such love is easy to come by? Do you imagine that it's only good when it's not tested?"

"We were tested. Many times." But nothing that hurt like this.

"My story is my own. I doubt that you wish to discuss yours, either. It only digs deeper, the more you think on it." Her expression relented. "I did not say forgiveness was simple. I realized, however, that if I had not allowed distance between us, he would not have strayed. I made him give up on me. Perhaps, however, you are completely innocent and your James fully evil."

"You know he's not. But—"

"No buts, *cara*. I did not say you would forget— either of you. Such a thing would be very nice. But there are trees that are scarred and grow bark over the wound and still live to provide shade and beauty. If your love is worth saving, you can do the same by working through this with him." She stepped away. "Or perhaps you prefer to decide that what you had is not worth the battle. You are free to make a new life and leave this one behind. You are a beautiful woman. There are men who will desire you."

Maybe before she'd remembered, she could have walked away from everyone without the tearing that she felt now, imagining living her life without the only real home she'd ever had.

Without the man who'd been that home.

She lifted brimming eyes to the older woman. "But I'm just so…angry." She stood. Paced. "So furious. I'd like to—"

"Slam a skillet up the side of his head?"

She couldn't help her choked laughter. "It's not funny."

"No." Luisa let her smile fade. "It is not. But throwing things is helpful, is it not?"

"I remembered that I have Italian blood."

"But of course." Luisa grinned again. "There is a spare set of dishes. I did not use them all on Romeo before he was lost to me."

Bella sobered. "I'm so sorry." She opened her arms. "I wish you could have him back."

Luisa accepted her embrace. "As do I. But you still have time with your James, God willing." She leaned back. "One can never be sure how much. And each day not savored is wasted."

Bella sighed, feeling drained by the whirlwind of emotions she'd experienced in less than a day.

"I have to talk to him." Urgency gripped her. "I have to find out where he is."

"Get dressed and eat. Your children are on the case. Your son is flying here to pick you up."

"When were you going to tell me?"

"When you returned to your senses and remembered the man who offered to give you up, if that's what you honestly wished."

"What? How do you know?"

"Dr. Sam. Your James told him that just before he left. But he threatened Dr. Sam if he should ever hurt you."

"James thinks I want...Sam? He *gave* me to Sam?" Fury raced past her worry. "Who does he think he is?"

"A man who is hurting. Who has lost his true love and believes that he cannot be forgiven." Luisa patted her cheek. "But who seeks to protect her still."

Her temper spiked even as her heart twisted.

The man was an idiot.

And too blasted noble for his own good.

"Maybe I'll borrow your skillet until I get home to mine," she said grimly.

Luisa chuckled. "I will help you pack."

CHAPTER TWENTY

WHEN THE PLANE taxied to the lone hangar, Cameron's grin was huge. He leaped from the pilot's seat and charged to her. "Mom! Is it true? Do you remember?"

She smiled. Cupped his cheek. "Not everything, not the accident, but you?" Her vision blurred. "How could I forget my baby boy?" She laughed when he winced. Opened her arms to him.

"You don't recall that we agreed no more of the baby-boy stuff?" But he was hugging her so hard she could barely breathe.

"I do," she said finally. "But you are my baby."

"Yeah, so deal, baby bro," sounded another voice from behind him.

"Oh!" Bella broke the hug. "I didn't see you, Muffin. How wonderful! Come here."

No hesitation from her daughter this time. Cele rushed into her embrace and held on tight. "Mama," was all she said. Her shoulders shook.

Bella snugged her daughter closer, then widened the circle to include Cam. So sweet, so unbearably precious to feel their love surround her.

Another bit of home.

At last, Cam spoke, his voice a little rough as he swiped at his eyes. "There's another storm system headed this way. We really should get going."

"Where is your father? Is he all right?"

Cam shifted. Shrugged.

Bella faced Cele. "Is he home?"

"As of this morning." The two exchanged glances.

"What aren't you saying?"

Finally, Cele answered. "He told us what happened. What he did. That you'd left him when you went on your trip. And when you remembered, you threw him out."

"I yelled at him," Cam admitted. "What an asshole."

"Don't speak of your father that way," Bella said sharply.

"But he—"

"What happened is between your father and me. It doesn't change our love for you one whit."

"Are you getting a divorce?" Ever the realist, Cele was the one to ask.

But she seemed a small girl again as she did.

How hard this must be for them, after all they'd been through, to have their hopes dashed. She'd remembered, as they'd longed for her to do…and because of it, they might lose their family yet.

"I can't say." At their crestfallen expressions, she continued, "I hope not." She'd progressed that far, at least.

"But things will have to change." That much she knew.

"They already are," Cam piped up.

Cele dug her elbow into his ribs. "Hush."

"What do you mean?"

"Not a thing," Cele said with a murderous glare at her sibling.

"Yeah. Uh, we should get going," he said.

"What are you hiding? Is he all right?"

"I don't think so." At Bella's gasp, Cele hastened to reassure her. "He's not physically hurt or anything, at least no more than he was when you last saw him."

At which point, he was more than a bit banged up. Sam was still limping around and sporting a huge shiner plus assorted scrapes and bruises.

"Explain what you mean, then."

Both shook their heads. "It's not our place, Mama," Cele said. "This is between you and Daddy."

True. Even if she could dig more out of them, in the final analysis, she and James had to work through their problems themselves.

"All right," she said, and squeezed them both. "Give me a minute to say goodbye to Luisa and Sam. Then let's go home."

Her children beamed with such hope that she played her part.

But she would only know for certain what she would do when she encountered James.

THE SENSE OF HOMECOMING was sharp and bitter-sweet. The sight of the house brought tears to her eyes. She'd lived in it with James for more than thirty-five years now. Before him, she'd never been in one spot for more than a matter of months.

They'd brought their babies home to this house. Fought and made up, dreamed and schemed and played beneath the wide, welcoming eaves.

Every bush and flower, each tree had felt the touch of her hands. She loved every brick and stick of this place.

But she didn't know if it would ever again be the refuge she remembered.

"He's so sad, Mama," Cele murmured.

Bella pressed her forehead against the window glass. "So am I, Muffin."

"Can you fix it?" Cam asked, sounding more like nine than nineteen.

"That isn't all up to me." She stepped out. Clasped the door handle. "But whatever happens between your father and me doesn't change how much we love you. I can't make promises, except that I will try." She smiled at their wistful faces, so young and worried, though her stomach was a bundle of nerves. "I love you both."

"Love you, too, Mama."

"You'll be okay?" Cam asked, as if he must protect her now.

"Of course." She blew them a kiss. "I'll call you." When they hesitated, she shooed with her fingers. "Go on."

She watched them leave, waving until they were out of view.

Then she set out to discover what would become of her life.

HE HADN'T SLEPT since he'd departed Lucky Draw. To work with power tools in such a state was beyond foolish.

But, he acknowledged wryly, he'd already been far more stupid.

He'd done a lot of thinking. Made some calls, set plans into motion. Then he'd needed to channel the nervous energy, so he'd put his hands to work while his mind churned.

He hadn't learned the craft of woodworking from his dad, who'd been content to run the plant and support his family. His grandfather had been the one to teach him, to see promise in him. They'd passed many hours together with these very tools, which James inherited when Granddad had died.

He'd tried out newer tools, but only the old ones felt truly right. At the moment, shaping the wood soothed him as nothing else ever had.

Except spending time with Bella.

He had to stop thinking about her. He forced his mind back to the piece he was finishing. How had he lost sight of what this did for him? For years and years, all his energies had been drained by running the plant, by plotting cash flow and liquidity ratios, inventorying stock or perusing orders.

Once he'd designed most of what they built. Made the prototypes himself. It had been nearly a decade since he'd even sketched out a piece, much less made one.

This felt good. Damn good.

"It's beautiful."

He dropped the sanding block, grateful he hadn't been operating a saw. He'd be minus a finger or two now.

Slowly, he turned.

And there she stood.

"It's you who's beautiful," he said, his voice gone husky.

An uncertain smile flashed at him, then vanished. He couldn't decide if he should be heartened by her nerves.

Before he could, she moved past him. Stroked the wood as he wondered if she'd ever stroke him again.

"You remembered." Her own voice was low and a little shaky.

"I'm sorry it's taken me so long to get to it." He shoved away from the workbench. "I'm so very sorry for everything."

"Don't. You've already said that."

He heard her tears. "What can I do, Bella? I'll say it a hundred times a day for the rest of my life if that's what you want. Do you need me to crawl? How can I make you understand that I don't know what the hell I was thinking, that I'd sell my soul to change it, but I can't. I can't, goddamn it, and that makes me sick. *I* make me sick because I hurt you, the most important person in my world, and we're going to lose everything, and it's my own blasted fault—" He snagged the sanding block, hurled it at the wall.

Dropped his head as his chest heaved. Felt his hope drain away at her silence.

He straightened, itching to move. To escape the agony.

But she was already at his back, curving herself against him. "It isn't all your fault," she said softly, and put her arms around his waist.

He shuddered with renewed hope. With relief that she was touching him. But he couldn't let himself off the hook that easily. "It is." He clasped her hands to keep her close but revolved in her arms. "It is."

"No. We lost each other, James. I'm not sure how. I was so afraid when we first met—"

"You?" He goggled. "You were fearless."

"When you've been tossed around from house to house, always the fifth wheel, the burden, you learn not to admit that you're scared or people will take advantage of it.

"But I was terrified all the time that you'd be like the others and change your mind. That the prince would get tired of the beggar girl. So I set out to make a home so strong, so invulnerable that nothing could ever threaten us. Where you'd be so happy that you wouldn't leave me the way everyone else had." Sorrow crept over her beloved features. "But it never dawned on me that we could be the threats ourselves.

Me, so sad after the kids left home, and you, belea-guered by the business." She lifted her gaze to his. "We went astray, James. We forgot what made us strong. And after all that happened, once I remem-bered again about—" she cleared her throat "—her, well, it was like the first days again. I was all by myself, unsure what would become of me. If anyone would ever give me a home."

"I am so—"

She hushed him with fingers across his lips. "No more sorrys, remember? If we're to have a chance—"

He gripped her. "Are we? Do you want to try again?"

"Luisa posed a question when I was so angry and hurt." She looked at him. "So afraid." After a mo-ment, she continued, "She challenged me to tally the pluses and minuses, even this big minus, and calcu-late how they would all balance out."

He was almost afraid to ask, but did anyway. "So how did I score?"

A quick grin, a faint flicker of her old mischief. "It took me a while. I was more interested in throw-ing dishes at the time."

"Did you?"

She nodded. "Luisa had a set she hadn't used up on her Romeo. I finished it off."

"And?"

She frowned. "I don't know how to forget what happened. The very thought of that woman with you makes me sick to my stomach." She placed one hand on his belly. "This body is mine." Her voice was a growl. "Mine, do you hear me? The idea of another woman's hands touching you, being touched—"

She shoved away. "If I think of it, I can't bear it. I'd like to kill her." She glared. "Sometimes I'd like to kill you."

His shoulders sank and he turned to go, but she grabbed his elbow. "I can't forget yet, James. Maybe I never will." Her voice wavered. "But I want to forgive you. I need to."

For a minute, what she'd said didn't register. He'd thought she was telling him they were through for certain, but then—

He wheeled. "Forgive me? Is that what you said?" All the world seem to go so still he could hear his heart pound.

She nodded. "I hate that it happened, hate it so much I can't breathe—but however furious I am, I could never hate you, James. If I'd paid more attention, if I hadn't been so absorbed in my own misery—"

He crushed her against him. Could not speak for the staggering relief rushing through him so fast his head was light.

Then he held her at arm's length. "I'm changing things. I've begun the process to step down. I'll have to work with Cele until she's ready, but I've already told everyone that she'll be assuming a greater share of responsibility. She's excited about it. And the second that it's possible, we're going on a long trip to visit all the places you've wanted to see. Do any crazy thing you've ever dreamed of."

Her eyes were wide and stunned. "What—I don't—" she blinked. "What are you saying?"

"That I love you, Bella. More than my life. More than anything or anyone in the world, and we're not putting off dreams one day longer than absolutely necessary. I hadn't realized what I'd done to you, not until you were gone. I trapped a butterfly and caged her. You were meant to fly, my love, not plod along with the ants."

"But—"

He herded her toward the glider that she'd wished for so often. "And neither am I—only, I never realized it. You freed me once, Bella, and I walked right back into the cell, dragging you with me. This is what I'm good at, not running the company."

"But the business. You love it."

"I love the history, but I was only a caretaker at heart. It's time for the next generation to step up. I was little older than Cele when I was put at the helm, and she's far better suited than me. I won't leave her until she's comfortable, but it won't be long, I promise you."

He swiveled her back to face him. "Will you wait for me? I swear I'll be home early every night, and we'll spend this time planning our travels. Then, when we've seen all you want, maybe we can return home and laze beneath the trees in this glider you've been wishing I'd build for years."

"Maybe I don't care about traveling anymore," she said.

"That's your decision. I've made mine. I'm getting back to what's important—you and me."

She fell silent. He forced himself to remain still, taking heart from her fingers caressing the wood of the glider.

"I don't feel like I'm really home yet." Her eyes welled. "I need to walk in my garden," she said. "Need to see our house."

Our house. He swallowed hard.

She extended a hand. "Come with me?"

"Anywhere." He clasped her fingers, and they began walking, her eyes busily drinking in the sights.

Abruptly she stopped. "There's just one thing missing."

He frowned. "What?"

"My ring." She glanced at him with a flicker of nerves. "Do you still have it?"

His heart leaped. "Absolutely." He didn't waste a second retrieving it from a chain around his neck. Slipping it on her finger.

For a long moment, she studied the circle of diamonds. Her gaze rose to his, bright with the love he'd feared never to see again. "Thank you, James."

"Thank you?" He goggled.

"No matter what happened before, it was you who helped me find the way home."

"Oh, love…" Throat thick, he drew her close. Kissed her with everything in him.

Then he swept her into his arms like a new bride and opened the door to their house.

To their new life.
He stepped over the threshold.
"Welcome home, butterfly."
Bella smiled, her heart wide open this time—
And the sun rose in James Parker's sky.

* * * * *

*Ladies, start your engines with a sneak preview
of Harlequin's officially licensed
NASCAR® romance series.*

Life in a famous racing family comes at a price

All his life Larry Grosso has lived in the shadow
of his well-known racing family—but it's now
time for him to take what he wants. And on top
of that list is Crystal Hayes—breathtaking,
sweet…and twenty-two years younger. But
their age difference is creating animosity within
their families, and suddenly their romance is the
talk of the entire NASCAR circuit!

*Turn the page for a sneak preview of
OVERHEATED
by Barbara Dunlop
On sale July 29 wherever books are sold.*

make the narrow parking lot entrance. So she pushed

Rufus, as Crystal Hayes had decided to call the black Lab, slept soundly on the soft seat even as she maneuvered the Softco truck in front of the Dean Grosso garage. Engines fired through the open bay doors, compressors clacked and impact tools whined as the teams tweaked their race cars in preparation for qualifying at the third race in Charlotte.

As always when she visited the garage area, Crystal experienced a vicarious thrill, watching the technicians' meticulous, last-minute preparations. As the daughter of a machinist, she understood the difference a fraction of a degree or a thousandth of an inch could make in the performance of a race car.

She muscled the driver's door shut behind her and waved hello to a couple of familiar crew members in their white-and-pale-blue jumpsuits. Then she rounded the back of the truck and rolled up the door. Inside, five boxes were marked Cargill Motors.

One of them was big and heavy, and it had slid forward a few feet, probably when she'd braked to make the narrow parking lot entrance. So she pushed up the sleeves of her canary-yellow T-shirt, then stretched forward to reach the box. A couple of catcalls came her way as her faded blue jeans tightened across her rear end. But she knew they were good-natured, and she simply ignored them.

She dragged the box toward her over the gritty metal floor.

"Let me give you a hand with that," a deep, melodious voice rumbled in her ear.

"I can manage," she responded crisply, not wanting to engage with any of the catcallers.

Here in the garage, the last thing she needed was one of the guys treating her as if she was something other than, well, one of the guys.

She'd learned long ago there was something about her that made men toss out pickup lines like parade candy. And she'd been around race crews long enough to know she needed to behave like a buddy, not a potential date.

She piled the smaller boxes on top of the large one.

"It looks heavy," said the voice.

"I'm tough," she assured him as she scooped the pile into her arms.

He didn't move away, so she turned her head to subject him to a *back off* stare. But she found herself staring into a compelling pair of green...no, brown... no, hazel eyes. She did a double take as they seemed to twinkle, multicolored, under the garage lights.

The man insistently held out his hands for the

boxes. There was a dignity in his tone and little crinkles around his eyes that hinted at wisdom. There wasn't a single sign of flirtation in his expression, but Crystal was still cautious.

"You know I'm being paid to move this, right?" she asked him.

"That doesn't mean I can't be a gentleman."

Somebody whistled from a workbench. "Go, Professor Larry."

The man named Larry tossed a "Back off" over his shoulder. Then he turned to Crystal. "Sorry about that."

"Are you for real?" she asked, growing uncomfortable with the attention they were drawing. The last thing she needed was some latter-day Sir Galahad defending her honor at the track.

He quirked a dark eyebrow in a question.

"I mean," she elaborated, "you don't need to worry. I've been fending off the wolves since I was seventeen."

"Doesn't make it right," he countered, attempting to lift the boxes from her hands.

She jerked back. "You're not making it any easier."

He frowned.

"You carry this box, and they start thinking of me as a girl."

Professor Larry dipped his gaze to take in the curves of her figure. "Hate to tell you this," he said, a little twinkle coming into those multifaceted eyes.

Something about his look made her shiver inside. It was a ridiculous reaction. Guys had given her the once-over a million times. She'd learned long ago to ignore it.

"Odds are," Larry continued, a teasing drawl in his tone, "they already have."

She turned pointedly away, boxes in hand as she marched across the floor. She could feel him watching her from behind.

* * * * *

Crystal Hayes could do without her looks,
men obsessed with her looks, and guys who think
they're God's gift to the ladies.
Would Larry be the one guy who could blow all
of Crystal's preconceptions away?
Look for OVERHEATED
by Barbara Dunlop.
On sale July 29, 2008.

REQUEST YOUR FREE BOOKS!

2 FREE NOVELS PLUS 2 FREE GIFTS!

◆ HARLEQUIN®

Super Romance®

Exciting, emotional, unexpected!

YES! Please send me 2 FREE Harlequin Superromance® novels and my 2 FREE gifts (gifts are worth about $10). After receiving them, if I don't wish to receive any more books, I can return the shipping statement marked "cancel." If I don't cancel, I will receive 6 brand-new novels every month and be billed just $4.69 per book in the U.S. or $5.24 per book in Canada, plus 25¢ shipping and handling per book and applicable taxes, if any*. That's a savings of close to 15% off the cover price! I understand that accepting the 2 free books and gifts places me under no obligation to buy anything. I can always return a shipment and cancel at any time. Even if I never buy another book from Harlequin, the two free books and gifts are mine to keep forever.

135 HDN EEX7   336 HDN EEYK

Name	(PLEASE PRINT)	
Address		Apt. #
City	State/Prov.	Zip/Postal Code

Signature (if under 18, a parent or guardian must sign)

Mail to the **Harlequin Reader Service:**
IN U.S.A.: P.O. Box 1867, Buffalo, NY 14240-1867
IN CANADA: P.O. Box 609, Fort Erie, Ontario L2A 5X3

Not valid to current subscribers of Harlequin Superromance books.

Want to try two free books from another line?
Call 1-800-873-8635 or visit www.morefreebooks.com.

* Terms and prices subject to change without notice. N.Y. residents add applicable sales tax. Canadian residents will be charged applicable provincial taxes and GST. Offer not valid in Quebec. This offer is limited to one order per household. All orders subject to approval. Credit or debit balances in a customer's account(s) may be offset by any other outstanding balance owed by or to the customer. Please allow 4 to 6 weeks for delivery. Offer available while quantities last.

Your Privacy: Harlequin is committed to protecting your privacy. Our Privacy Policy is available online at www.eHarlequin.com or upon request from the Reader Service. From time to time we make our lists of customers available to reputable third parties who may have a product or service of interest to you. If you would prefer we not share your name and address, please check here. ☐

HSR08R

Silhouette®

Romantic
SUSPENSE

Sparked by Danger,
Fueled by Passion.

Cindy Dees
Killer Affair

Seduction in the sand…and a killer on the beach.

Can-do girl Madeline Crummby is off to a remote
Fijian island to review an exclusive resort, and she hires
Tom Laruso, a burned-out bodyguard, to fly her there
in spite of an approaching hurricane. When their plane
crashes, they are trapped on an island with a serial killer
who stalks overaffectionate couples. When their false
attempts to lure out the killer turn all too real, Tom and
Madeline must risk their lives and their hearts….

**Look for the third installment
of this thrilling miniseries,
available August 2008
wherever books are sold.**

HARLEQUIN *Super Romance*

COMING NEXT MONTH

#1506 MATTHEW'S CHILDREN • C.J. Carmichael
Three Good Men

Rumor at their law firm cites Jane Prentice as the reason for Matthew Gray's divorce. The truth is, however, Jane avoids him—and not because he's a single dad. But when they're assigned to the same case, will they be able to ignore the sparks between them?

#1507 NOT ON HER OWN • Cynthia Reese
Count on a Cop

His uncle lost his best farmland to a crook, and now Brandon Wilkes is losing his heart and his pride to the crook's granddaughter…who refuses to leave the land her grandfather stole from them! How can he possibly be friends with Penelope Langston?

#1508 A PLACE CALLED HOME • Margaret Watson
The McInnes Triplets

It was murder in self-defense, and Zoe McInnes thinks she's put her past behind her. Until the brother of her late husband shows up, and Gideon Tate's own issues make him determined to seek revenge. Not even her sisters can help Zoe out of this mess. Besides, she thinks maybe Gideon is worth all the trouble he's putting her through…and more.

#1509 MORE THAN A MEMORY • Roz Denny Fox
Going Back

Seven years ago Garret Logan was devastated when his fiancée, Colleen, died in a car accident. He's tried to distract himself with work, but he hasn't been able to break free of her memory. Until the day she walks back into his pub with a new name, claiming not to remember him…

#1510 WORTH FIGHTING FOR • Molly O'Keefe
The Mitchells of Riverview Inn

Jonah Closky will do anything for his mom. That's the only reason he's at this inn to meet his estranged father and brothers. Still, there is an upside to being here: Daphne Larson. With the attraction between them, he can't think of a better way to pass the time.

#1511 SAME TIME NEXT SUMMER• Holly Jacobs
Everlasting Love

When tragedy strikes Carolyn Kendal's daughter, it's Carolyn's first love, Stephan Foster, who races to her side. A lifetime of summers spent together has taught them to follow their hearts. But after so much time apart—and the reappearance of her daughter's father—will their hearts lead them to each other?